THE NEON HAYSTACK

THE NEON HAYSTACK

JAMES MICHAEL ULLMAN

WILDSIDE PRESS

Published by Wildside Press LLC.
www.wildsidebooks.com

BOOK ONE: APRIL

CHAPTER 1

The jet banked to the left and I looked down and there it was, a splash of steel and wood and concrete rising from the plain. The day was cloudless, the air clear. Below me a million people were going about their business. And as the jet descended, gliding down like a frozen bird, the details of the mosaic below emerged—streets and highways, cars and trucks, rooftops, human beings.

For a moment, sitting there with the low whine of the engines in my ears, I experienced fear and doubt. A man could spend a lifetime and still never search every corner of that city and its environs. The city proper alone covered more than a hundred square miles. And the suburbs fanned endlessly into the prairie.

And then I thought: Knock it off, Kolchak. You're a bullhead, remember? Too dumb to fear, too stupid to doubt. Only a bullhead could carry out the Master Plan. So never doubt again.

When the jet landed, I was the first passenger off.

His name was Max Fuller. The sign on his office door said he was a private investigator. He did not look like a private investigator. He was fat and old and bald. His nose was a shapeless purple blob. He wore a nondescript, rumpled, shiny blue suit. Gravy spots decorated his ancient, wide-flaring necktie. His eyes were rheumy. The first and second fingers of his right hand had been stained yellow by tobacco.

As I entered, Max Fuller looked up from behind his desk and smiled benignly, like a shorn Santa Claus. He said in a startlingly deep, hoarse voice, "You must be the man from Arabia. Just clump your bags in a corner. I presume you got my reply."

I said, "I did."

I set my bags down and pulled up a chair. I flopped and lit a cigarette.

Blandly, Max Fuller gazed at me for a moment and then said, "Confidentially, I think you're a damn fool."

"Then you won't help me?"

"Oh, I'll help you. If you insist. But I think you are about to engage in a colossal waste of time and money." The detective opened his desk drawer. He extracted a cigar. Slowly he peeled the wrapping away. "Your letter from Arabia neglected to mention who gave you my name. I'm just curious. I don't recall any Arabs among my satisfied customers."

I smiled. "He wasn't an Arab. Years ago, he used to be an assistant state's attorney in this city. Now he's a high-ranking trouble-shooter for an international oil company."

"That would be Barney. What'd he tell you? That I'm the best private dick in town?"

"No. Only that you're probably the only completely honest private dick in town."

Fuller chuckled. "Good old Barney. I should warn you, though. My license has been suspended nine times and twice it was nearly revoked." He glanced around the tiny room. The walls were cracked. One of the ceiling bulbs was out. "But as you can see, I haven't made much money. My poverty is mute testimony to my good character. No divorce cases. No industrial spying. No wire taps, and no electronic bugs under subjects' beds. Nevertheless, despite those restrictions, I've led an interesting professional life."

He lit his cigar. Smoke billowed about him in great clouds. "However," he went on, "in my letter of reply to you, I wasn't kidding. I'm too old for anything big or active any more. I'm semiretired. I just putter around with routine personnel and character investigations, nothing more. And I go home at three every afternoon for a warm bath and a nap. Doctor's orders."

"Barney told me that too. But that's all I want. Routine character investigations. I'll tell you which characters to investigate."

"Your letter said you wanted my connection with you kept secret."

"That's right. You'll be my secret service. I don't even want to see you again except in emergency. But I do need your help. Or someone like you, who knows this city, has contacts, and can collect routine background data fast."

"Okay. Each time you find someone you want me to investigate, print the name and identification on a plain piece of paper and mail it to me. After I make the check, I'll mail the reports to you, in envelopes apparently containing advertising promotion junk. That's in case someone peeks in your mailbox to spot letterheads. That way, we'll also avoid telephones. In my business, I've learned to distrust them."

"Suppose an emergency arises?"

"Call here first. Identify yourself as 'Mr. Kay.' If you don't get an answer, dial this number." Fuller scrawled a number on a slip of paper. He handed it to me. "Memorize that, and destroy the paper. It's my unlisted home phone. I have the line checked for taps each month, just as I do my office line. My wife will answer. She always knows where I am, at any hour. Frankly, I think you're over-concerned with secrecy. And I'm still unhappy about taking your fee for this job. The only reason I'm taking it is, if I don't, someone else will, and they'd probably stick you for an even higher fee. But if you are worried about secrecy, let me give you some general advice: Always call from a public phone. Never say anything to anyone you wouldn't want overheard except on a public phone. Preferably a public phone you've never used before. And never, under any circumstances, go through a switchboard."

"Thanks."

I stubbed my cigarette out. I rose.

"By the way," Fuller said, "if there's ever any person of importance in this town you're not allowed to talk to, or any place you're not allowed to enter, don't hesitate to ask my assistance. For you, it's part of the service. While I haven't made much money, I have made some friends. I may be able to open doors, with a two-minute phone call, that you couldn't batter down in a week."

"I'll remember that."

"Where will you be?"

"For now, the Moreland. But I'll move soon to a place near."

"You plan to pursue this insanity very long?"

"If necessary," I said, "for a year. Or more."

Fuller blinked. He cleared his throat. He said, "Well, good luck. And be careful."

I checked in at the Moreland Hotel a little before 7 p.m.

At first I didn't attract much attention. A bellboy picked up my bags at the curb. I strolled through the lobby like any other new guest. It was a big lobby, tastefully furnished, as any establishment charging the Moreland's rates should be furnished.

My anonymous status changed when I reached the desk. I said to the clerk, "I'm Mr. Kolchak. I have a reservation. Room 703."

The clerk's right hand, in the act of extending a pen, trembled slightly. For this clerk, it was an impressive show of emotion.

He said, "Mr. *Kolchak*. Oh, yes. We were expecting you, sir.

He said it loud enough for two other men behind the desk to hear. They both turned and stared.

Ignoring them, I signed the register.

The clerk banged a bell.

"Boy," he said, reaching for a key, "703. For Mr. *Kolchak*."

The boy almost dropped my bags.

I looked at the boy and asked, "Is your name Maurice Shevlin?"

"No, sir," the boy said. He was a cool one. He picked up the bags and held his face straight. He said, "Maurice, he left. He's in the army now."

"Then you'll do," I said.

We marched to the elevator. Behind the desk, more hotel employees came out to gape.

The boy and I rode up to seven in silence. The attractive Puerto Rican girl at the controls made a great show of pretending I wasn't there.

When we reached 703, the boy went through all the motions. He put my bags down, turned on a couple of lights, and opened the bathroom door to prove the room was equipped with a toilet.

I tipped him fifty cents.

"I'd like," I said, "a bottle of cold beer. Think you could find one?"

"Call room service," the boy suggested. He left in a hurry.

I called room service. Then I removed my topcoat and hung it in the closet. I took my suit jacket off and hung that up, too. I walked to the window and peered out at a park across the street. For April, the evening was unseasonably warm. Just as it had been unseasonably cold the April night a year earlier when my brother had peered out that same window. This evening several of the park benches were occupied. The Moreland was about a mile from the main business district, in a well-to-do residential section of the city. The people in the park looked well dressed and well fed.

I loosened my tie, rolled up my sleeves, and stepped into the bathroom. I splashed cold water on my face. The face of a 35-year-old bullhead. Steve Kolchak. A guy with curly black hair, a low brow, a wide nose, big lips, and a thick jaw. A guy who always needed a shave. Whose shoulders were broad, and whose arms, legs, and torso were thick. Who stood 5'9" and weighed 185 and had played guard on the high-school football team.

That was me. Steve Kolchak, world traveler out of Gary, Indiana, thanks to the fact he'd barely acquired a degree in construction engineering and had some knowledge of how to build bridges, dams, barracks, and airfields. The original boomer, a dumb slob with no entanglements, no dependents, no responsibilities.

And now, without even a kid brother. Which was why I had come to this city in the first place.

A man from room service brought the beer half an hour later. He must have walked to the brewery for it.

I handed him a dollar bill. That covered the price of premium beer in this hotel, plus a ten-cent tip for him.

"Thanks a million," I said. "I sure do appreciate promptness."

"Yessir," the man said. He scooted out without so much as a sneer.

I downed about half the bottle while sprawled in a blond-wood chair. I was gazing at a cowboy slaughtering other cowboys on the room's television set when someone rapped smartly on the door.

I put my glass down. I sighed. This was bound to come sooner or later. The question was: In a situation like this, who would they send?

I got up, lumbered to the door, and opened it.

At first glance, I pegged the man who stood gazing down at me as the owner of the hotel. He dressed well enough to own the Moreland. The subdued blue sports jacket had set him back close to a hundred. The gray slacks were straight from the British Isles. The single-toned silk neckpiece represented a minimum of ten dollars. The black loafers were soft leather; the equally black hat was high-grade felt.

But then, I reflected, the Moreland was probably owned by a syndicate of investors or by a corporation, not by one man. What's more, this man was lean and hard. He towered five inches over me, but his weight must have been about the same as mine. His face was thin, his jaw round but strong. His unblinking gray eyes sized me up in one second with disconcerting thoroughness. His nose, straight and unmarred, hung over narrow lips that curved in an implacable smile.

"Mr. Kolchak?"

"That's right."

"My name's Doyle. Van Doyle. I'm a lieutenant of police." Casually, he put a manicured hand into his breast pocket and extracted a wallet, which he flipped open.

Sure enough. The star was unmistakably genuine.

"May I come in?"

"Of course."

I walked back to my chair and sat down. Doyle followed me partway into the room. He removed his hat. His hair was light gray. Putting his hair and his face together, I estimated his age at forty.

I asked, "What can I do for you?"

"I'm just inquisitive."

"What about?"

"About why you want to frighten the people who work in this hotel. They don't know anything. They just work here."

"I'm sorry. But I wanted to do everything my kid brother did. I think I'm entitled to do that."

"It would have helped," Doyle said, "if you'd explained that in your letter asking for reservations in Room 703."

"I was in a hurry. And after all, what's so terrible about my writing and asking for a reservation in the same room my brother had a year ago?"

"I don't deny your right to do it. I just think you could have done it differently."

"Are you Sergeant Morrissey's superior?"

Doyle sat down on the bed. His unblinking eyes never left me. "No. Morrissey works in Missing Persons. I work out of the Clay Street Precinct."

"The Moreland is a long way from Clay Street, isn't it?"

"It is. But your brother was last seen on Clay Street. That made it my job. And while Morrissey's group has technical jurisdiction of a sort, I take a personal interest in everything that happens on Clay Street. And I follow through to the end."

I finished the beer. I said, "I wrote Morrissey, you know. I told him I was coming to this city as soon as my contract in Arabia expired. I told him I'd check in at the Moreland. As a matter of fact, I telephoned him last week from New York and asked if he'd learned any thing more."

"I haven't talked to Morrissey in six months. But the people at this hotel called me last week and said they'd received your request for a reservation. For Room 703. They called me again this evening and said you'd turned up. Which is why I'm here. Because the police have enough trouble of their own, without a well-meaning private citizen like yourself interfering with police business."

I leaned over and flipped the television set off. I settled back in the chair.

"That's rich. 'Police business.' Look, man. You've had a year in which to learn what happened to my brother. You haven't learned a damn thing. It's pretty obvious now you've given it up as a bad deal. As far as my brother's case is concerned, you're through."

"That's not true."

"Isn't it? How many men are working full-time on the case this very minute?"

Doyle didn't reply.

"That's what I thought. Nobody. Just a couple guys now and then. And the usual routine check on the pawn shops for my brother's stuff. Now that's fine, Doyle. Keep it up. I'm not complaining, I couldn't expect more. Not of your police department, nor of any police department in the world. But don't try to pretend my brother's case is still getting top priority."

The lieutenant pulled a cigarette from his shirt pocket. He lit it with a twenty-dollar silver lighter.

He bared his pearly teeth and exhaled and said in a flat, unemotional voice, "I've about had it with you. We did everything we could. That's something you irate private citizens never try to understand. And the last thing we need now is a jerk big brother from Arabia barging into town, making like his brother's ghost and scaring the daylights out of everyone in the Moreland Hotel. Won't the newspapers have fun!"

"I'm afraid," I said, "I didn't just barge into town. I came here after considerable deliberation. And I plan to stay a long time."

"What for?"

"To do what you can't do. Find my kid brother, Ed Kolchak. Or, at least, find out what happened to him."

"You think we didn't try? You've seen Morrissey's reports. We talked to everyone. We put the screws on all our Clay Street informants. And came up with nothing."

"I don't doubt that. But there's not much more you can do now. You have other cases to solve. But me—I intend to work on my brother's case full-time."

"What can you investigate that we didn't? As far as any logical place to even start an investigation is concerned, your brother's case is a classic study in futility. He'd never been in this city before. He didn't know a soul here. He was a salesman for a structural steel company in Chicago, and he'd made an appointment by long-distance phone with the purchasing agent for a big manufacturing company. The appointment was for nine a.m. the morning of April tenth last year. Your brother arrived in this city April ninth on the six o'clock flight. He took a cab to the Moreland, where he checked into Room 703—this room. He ordered a bellboy, a lad named Maurice Shevlin, to bring him a bottle of beer. He'd eaten dinner on the plane. Apparently he spent an hour or so organizing his sales material. Then he went down to the lobby and stopped at the cigar counter. He bought an inexpensive street guide and also picked up a free entertainment guide. He inquired as to the distance to Clay Street, which is our city's version of glitter gulch—the French Quarter, Greenwich Village, Rush Street, and skid row all in one. He left the hotel a little before nine p.m. He took a cab from the stand in front of this hotel to the intersection of Clay and Jackson. He got out and paid the driver. The driver is the last person known to have seen him. That's all we learned, and that's all you'll learn. So why don't you go back to Arabia?"

"Because Ed's my brother," I said, "and the only family I have left in the world. That might not mean much to you or to most people these days, but it means a helluva lot to me. Like with the ancient Greeks, see? A matter of family honor. Or is that over your head?"

The detective gazed at his flawless shoes. Then he looked up, his eyes suddenly veiled.

"All right. I see I'm getting nowhere. Just bear in mind, a million people live in this city. And the trail is a year old. A year in which people can forget, in which evidence fades away."

"That passage of time," I said, "may work to my advantage. Ed wasn't naked when he stepped out of that cab, you know. He wore clothes and carried objects. His wallet, with his identification and credit cards..."

"We're still waiting for someone to try using one of those credit cards. But nobody has. Nobody tried to cash any of the traveler's checks he carried either."

"I know. But Ed had other things on him."

"Junk. Mostly unidentifiable. Except for the ring and the watch. The pawn shops are still alerted to that ring. And the watch—from the outside, it looks like a million other two-dollar watches."

"All the same, I'm going to put ads in the papers. Maybe since the publicity over my brother's disappearance died away, someone found one of those articles and doesn't realize its significance."

Doyle shrugged. "It's your money." He took a drag on his cigarette. "Did it ever occur to you that you might not want to know the truth about what happened to your brother? Clay Street is a nasty place. Maybe your brother had some nasty ideas when he went down there. A stranger alone on Clay Street can get into all sorts of trouble. And your brother—twenty-eight years old, in a city where nobody knew him…"

"Those implications don't scare me," I replied evenly. "And you know yourself there's nothing to them. You must have asked the Chicago police to check into Ed's habits. Ed traveled a lot, and when he traveled, he liked to scout out areas like Clay Street. Hell, he was no puritan, why shouldn't he? Ed was a personable guy. His technique in a new town was to hit a couple quiet little spots, where the natives most likely hung out. He'd strike up a conversation with the bartender or some customer, and in thirty minutes he'd have enough information to write a guidebook. He'd know which places to avoid, and which were worth taking in. Anyhow, Ed had an appointment with that purchasing agent at nine the next morning. He took his business seriously. I don't think he planned to stay down on Clay Street for long. I think he just intended to have a drink or two, get the feel of the area, and then return to the hotel early."

"Maybe your brother wanted to disappear."

I shook my head. "No dice. He corresponded with me regularly, and I've written to his employers and his friends. There was absolutely no hint of serious personal troubles. As a matter of fact, things had never been going better for him. He was making good money for a guy his age. He had a master's in engineering, and he knew how to sell to high-level technical executives. He led a full social life in Chicago. Girls—Ed had his pick. You might say he was the perfect bachelor."

Doyle got up. He seemed unhappy.

"I don't suppose you'd bother confiding to the police what you plan to do."

"I don't mind at all. Tonight I'll take a cab to Clay and Jackson. I'll get out and start walking around. I'll do that tomorrow night and every night until I've hit every establishment on or near Clay Street. I'll ask questions wherever I go. And after I hit every joint once, I'll go back and do it a second time. And a third. And so on."

"Now, that's a brilliant idea," Doyle said sarcastically. "Clay Street is loaded with human vermin of both sexes who'd slit a stranger's throat for a twenty-dollar bill. And if you pester them with questions night after night, they'll consider slitting your throat for nothing."

I pushed myself out of the chair. I led Doyle to the door.

"I'll risk it," I said. "By the way, if you want to reassure the Moreland's management about my presence, you might tell them I won't be staying more than a week. I'll find a place near Clay Street as soon as I can."

"If you do learn anything," Doyle said, "I hope you'll remember to tell us about it. No matter what you think, we're just as anxious to find your brother as you are."

"Of course."

Doyle left.

I sat down at the desk. I pulled a piece of paper from a pad.

On it I printed,

LT. VAN DOYLE. CLAY STREET PRECINCT.

I folded the paper once and slipped it into an envelope which I addressed to Max Fuller.

CHAPTER 2

The elevator girl who took me down was the same one who'd ferried me up. She planted her round little backside to me and stood at rigid attention, eyes straight ahead.

As we reached the lobby level I said, "Boo!"

She jumped as though goosed. She opened the door in a hurry.

At the cigar counter I bought a street guide and picked up a free entertainment guide. I didn't inquire as to the distance to Clay Street, though. I already knew that.

I also bought a stamp. The envelope to Max Fuller, I dropped into a mailbox.

Outside, I told the doorman, "I called the cab company. I asked to see the driver of Cab 444 in front of this hotel at nine o'clock."

The doorman, big, fat, and middle-aged, looked me right in the eye. He recognized me, but he, at least, didn't give a damn.

"Four-forty-four's parked across the street, sir. I suggested he wait there so he wouldn't block the line. I knew you'd want to see him."

"Thanks. You tell him who I was?"

"No."

I tipped the doorman a dollar.

The driver of Cab 444 was squinting at the financial page of an evening newspaper as I approached. I opened the back door and climbed in.

He turned. "Sorry." His face was round, his nose big and warped. He wore rimless glasses and his broad smile seemed sincere. I estimated his age at forty-five. "I can't take you anywhere. The cab is engaged."

"I'm the party who engaged you. I want a ride to the corner of Clay and Jackson."

"I don't get it. Any cab could haul you to Clay Street."

"I wanted you. You're Sam Alban, aren't you?"

"Look," Alban said genially, "if some joker told you I can find girls or a circus, you got the wrong guy. I take fares to Clay Street and let 'em out, that's all. What happens afterward is their business."

"I've got the right guy. A joker didn't tell me about you. The police did. They said you drove my kid brother to Clay Street a year ago."

Alban studied me. He nodded. "That one. Sure. He went to Clay and Jackson, too. I ought to remember him." The driver put his newspaper aside. "I talked to a hundred cops about it. Reporters followed me around.

You look a little like him. Only he was taller and thinner. You must be the older brother I read about. His only relative, it said."

"That's right. And I've come to this city to find Ed. So let's get going. I want you to let me out at the exact spot you let Ed out."

Alban started the cab. He steered slowly into traffic.

I asked, "What did my brother do during the ride?"

"He talked at first. He asked me to let him out in the middle of things. I told him it was a week night and with the weather so miserable cold, there probably wouldn't be much going on. He said that was all right, he'd see what he could find. Then he asked me about the joints down there, but I told him I didn't know Clay Street. A lot of drivers will tout some place and the doorman or a bartender pay 'em a buck or two a head. But I don't go for that. So then your brother, he just looked out the window."

Alban paused. "I told the cops that, too. They didn't believe me. They started shoving me around, in a back room at the Clay Street Precinct. They claimed I touted your brother to a dive and was afraid to admit it. So I hollered for a lie test. And you know what? They gave me a lie test and I passed."

"I know. I was overseas, but I kept up with the case."

"You think you'll learn more than the police found out?"

"I have more time than the police have. They work on a lot of cases at once. This is the only case I'm interested in. And my motives are more personal."

Like Ed, I spent the remainder of the ride looking out the window. Alban had nothing more to say either. He seemed pensive.

Cab 444 pulled to the curb. Alban cut the engine.

"Here it is."

"How much?"

"A buck-sixty."

I handed him two dollars. "Keep the change."

'Your brother did that, too. Just that way."

"I realize it's unlikely, but if you ever hear anything about my brother, I plan to be in town for some time. I won't be at the Moreland long, but I'll leave a forwarding address."

"Sure."

I held out my right hand, palm down. "See that ring?" The stone gleamed under the street light. "My brother wore one just like it. There are only two in the world—my brother's ring and mine. I had them made up in Tokyo. If you ever pick up a fare wearing a ring like this, I'd like to know. You might tell your buddies about it, too." I reached into my pocket. I gave Alban a small piece of paper. "Here's a mimeographed copy of the design. It's the Japanese character for brotherhood."

I opened the door.

"Mr. Kolchak…"

"Yes?"

"Well, I hope everything turns out all right. I really do. And you probably heard it before, but watch your step. Clay Street is rough. The Syndicate runs this part of town. The district police captain got his job through the ward committeeman. The committeeman is a Syndicate stooge. The fix runs all the way up through City Hall to the state legislature. That's why Clay Street is wide open."

"Thanks. I appreciate your concern."

"If you want, I can pick you up later and drive you back to the Moreland."

I shook my head. "I don't know how long I'll be. But tell you what. I plan to visit Clay Street every night. Why don't you pick me up tomorrow at the Moreland. At three in the afternoon." I smiled. "You can be my transportation corps."

"I'll be there."

I climbed out of the cab and closed the door. Alban drove away.

I stood alone, at Clay and Jackson, just as Edmund L. Kolchak had stood there twelve months earlier.

A brisk, warm wind tumbled scraps of paper down the gutter at my feet. Raucous phrases of music rose behind the traffic sounds—a brassy trumpet, a mourning clarinet. Signs glittered, THE DEN. EXOTIQUE. HIDEAWAY, CHEZ NANETTE. LEO'S. And of course girls…

Clay Street. Just as Ed had viewed it. Only this night Clay Street was crowded. No arctic current swept over the city from the northwest as it had the night Ed stood here. This night, the abnormally warm weather had roused all the denizens. Tired, foggy-eyed old men and bitter young men in rags and work clothes. A few wide-eyed, beardless boys from the suburbs and many cold-eyed, beardless boys from the slum. Small-town conventioneers, with more money than brains, mingling with the underworld's fringe. And always, hungry eyes on the women: occasional squaws and mountaineers in jeans, Puerto Ricans and Cubans in flowered print skirts, whores of every color and description, slummers in the latest fashions, and now and then a working girl or housewife hurrying to the residential or Bohemian sections nearby. A street financed by ruthless entrepreneurs and gathering in its backwash every element of the city's dispossessed. I had seen Clay Streets the world over. This one would be little different.

And now I had four choices. I could go north or south on Clay, or I could go east or west on Jackson. On Clay, lights beckoned; on Jackson, they gave way to rows of ancient apartment buildings.

I thought: Come on, bullhead. You've got to begin somewhere. After the first place, the others will be easy. So let's start effecting the Master Plan. Let's show the world how stubborn you can be.

I entered an all-night diner at 1201 North Clay, the northeast corner of Clay and Jackson. The waitress refused to talk to me. The short-order cook told me damned if he knew who walked by at this hour a year ago. He'd been in Peoria then and the waitress had been in Memphis, and if I didn't want to order anything, scram.

I dropped a sketch of the ring insignia on the counter. An old man drinking coffee picked it up, shrugged, crumpled it, and tossed it over his shoulder. Twelve wary eyes followed me out the door.

By eleven o'clock I'd reached the 1400 block. I'd stopped at two drugstores, a cafeteria, and nine bars. Two prostitutes tried to solicit me and three bartenders threatened to throw me out bodily. But here and there people did listen. Nobody remembered Ed. Most everybody remembered the case, though. It had been the talk of the street at the time.

At 11:35 p.m. I walked into a clip joint at 1427 North Clay called Kelly's club. On a small stage a tall dark-haired woman removed her clothes while performing a casual travesty of a dance. A heavy-eyed Negro thumped in a bored way on a drum as the woman peeled off her gown, spread her arms and legs, and rolled her hips. The two other bandsmen yawned. The tables and chairs ringing the stage were empty. The bar, however, was filled, since drinks there cost less. The patrons were all male, some fairly well dressed and others in leather jackets. Stonily, the men gazed at the stage.

A pale-faced greeter in a soiled tuxedo asked me if I'd like a table up front. I said no, I'd take a table in back. I settled in an uncomfortable chair beside the wall. The greeter faded from view before I could question him. That was all right. I'd catch him on the way out. For the moment I wanted a drink. I'd just left a strangely quiet little den patronized by a few scowling women garbed in mannish suits.

A waitress in a low-cut white blouse and skin-tight red pants said, "What'll you have, honey?"

I asked for beer. While the waitress got it, an exhausted blonde shoved herself from the bar, walked over, and asked if I wanted company. I said no, I'd drink alone. The blonde had expected that. Expressionless she returned to her post to await a live one.

While the waitress poured the beer I held out my right hand.

"Ever see a man wearing a ring like that?"

"Can't say that I did."

"Ever see a man who looked something like me? Only he was taller and younger. That's my brother."

"I see so many. I wouldn't know."

I gave her a sketch of the ring design. "Just keep this handy, hey, and watch for a man wearing that ring. Show it to your friends. I'll be around again."

"Sure, dear." She slipped the paper into her brassiere. "I really will."

She went back to the bar and said something to the bartender. The bartender reached for a telephone alongside his cash register and dialed a number.

Slowly I drank the beer. My feet hurt. It was a relief to sit down. Before long, I'd need a high-quality pair of hiking shoes.

The bottle was near-empty when a middle-aged man entered alone from the street. In an unhurried way, he headed straight for me. He wore a well-pressed blue suit and a subdued gray tie. He was balding, but he still sported a few strands of black hair. Of medium height, his shoulders were broad and his stomach was just comfortably rounded. An expression of studied cordiality masked his squarish face. His cheekbones were high. His nose was heavy, and his mouth wide. His blue eyes seemed remarkably bright, as though he'd just hopped out of an icy shower.

He halted about a foot from my table.

"You mind, Kolchak, if I join you?"

The voice was resonant and consciously modulated, as though the man had become aware relatively late in life of how he sounded to others. It figured.

"Not at all."

He pulled up another chair, his back to the stage. Still watching me, he raised his right hand and snapped his fingers.

He said, "I'll buy you a drink. Good stuff, not the crap the customers get. The very best bonded. Or anything else you like. I own this place, see."

Deferentially, the waitress loomed at his elbow. Like an obedient slave. Which, in fact, she probably was.

"Bourbon is fine. On the rocks."

"Two bourbons, Lucille."

Lucille hurried off.

I said, "You're Kelly, then."

"Oh, no." He smiled. "My name's Amber. It used to be something else, a name a lot like yours, but I shortened it. My friends call me Phil. And this ain't the only place I own. I got eleven places on Clay Street, for all kinds of customers. You were in one of the other dumps an hour ago, on the thirteen-hundred block. And I got many additional business interests."

"You seem pretty well informed on who I am and where I've been."

"By now," he said, "just about everyone on Clay Street knows who you are and where you been. This is a funny little community. We all compete for a buck. The American Way, see. But sometimes we pool information, like what they call a trade association. And so it's no secret no more that you're on Clay Street, looking for your lost brother."

"I see. In other words, you've been elected as the spokesman for this trade association. To learn what I'm up to."

"Something like that."

The drinks came. Phil Amber sipped his. I didn't touch mine.

"Very well. I'll tell you the word to spread along your communications network. You can say I intend to go on looking for my brother until I know what happened to him. I'm going to do every night what I did tonight. I'm going to stop at every establishment that's open and ask questions. If necessary, I'll do that for a year or more. I've saved enough money to finance the venture that long at least. And when my money runs out, who knows? I might get a job in this city and keep plugging away part-time. I'm a construction engineer and I saw a lot of building going on as the plane landed this afternoon."

Amber considered this.

"I don't think," he concluded thoughtfully, "it'll work. If a guy did know anything about your brother, he'd stay away from you. Knowing you were on Clay Street, he'd stay away from Clay Street. The cops had a lot of pressure put on them when your brother disappeared. From reformers and so forth, who like to put the heat on Clay Street for political reasons. Big stories in the newspapers. Things were so bad that for a while my dancers weren't even allowed to bare their breasts, and you know what that can do to business in a dump like this one. And so some of us, in our trade association, we asked a few questions too. We figured that if your brother was found, the reformers would lay off. But we didn't learn no more than the police learned."

I picked up my drink. I downed some of it.

"You can't change my mind."

"I wouldn't try," Amber said. "But I oughta warn you. A lot of businessmen on Clay Street don't like strangers who ask questions. Only the cops can get away with that. And when the newspapers get wind of what you're up to, there'll be more stories about your brother's disappearance, and all the bad things that are supposed to happen down here."

I shook my head. "I don't think anyone will hurt me. They wouldn't dare. You wouldn't let 'em. Think what a story that would make—'Man Knifed On Clay Street While Seeking Lost Brother.' You'd never allow that to happen, Mr. Amber. You know that while the newspapers will make a big thing of my being here, I'll be just a one-day sensation. But that if I'm roughed up or killed, the heat will go on more than ever."

Amber smiled. "That's very good." He finished his drink. "We wondered if you'd be smart enough to figure that out. And I told my associates you were a college man, you'd been all over the world, you wouldn't be bluffed. Okay. We don't like you here, but so long as you don't get out of line, there's nothing we can do about it. Personally, I think you'll get tired of beating your head against a wall. You'll go back to building bridges. Either that, or hanging around in these dumps, you'll turn into an alcoholic. You won't get no more free drinks from me, though."

He pushed his chair back.

"So go on looking. But remember, I ain't responsible for everyone on Clay Street. There's a lot goes on here I don't know and don't want to know, even where my own associates are concerned. So I'm not guaranteeing you'll lead a charmed life."

"Thanks for the bourbon."

"Don't mention it." Amber's eyes strayed to the bar. "By the way, you're being followed."

"By whom?"

"Two detectives from the Clay Street Precinct. The two young guys in black jackets, dressed like truck drivers. They picked you up in the seventh place you hit. Doyle is the night lieutenant, I guess he decided to give you a bodyguard. But if you keep this up every night, he'll have to pull your bodyguard off. He's short on manpower as it is."

* * * *

Two men hopped from a parked car as I left Kelly's Club. Both wore sports coats and one carried a camera.

"That must be him," the man with the camera said.

The other man walked up to me. He was tall, blond, and bare-headed, about thirty years old. His face was thin and amiable. He asked, "You're Stephen Kolchak, aren't you? The lost guy's brother?"

"That's right."

"I'm Bill Totten. A reporter for the Beacon. We got a tip from some bartender you were down here. How long you been in town?"

A crowd, attracted by the photographer's press camera, began to gather.

"Since this afternoon."

"What are you doing?"

"Looking for Ed."

"Where are you staying?"

"The Moreland. Same room Ed had."

"How long you plan to be here?"

"Until I find my brother. However long that takes."

"Oh boy," the reporter said. "Mind if we grab a few pictures?"

I let them have their fun. The sooner the first flurry of excitement about my presence on Clay Street ended, the better. Meanwhile, the stories in the press might turn up someone who had seen the ring or the watch.

I was photographed supposedly questioning panhandlers, bartenders, and B-girls who agreeably hiked their tight skirts to their thighs. Partway through Totten's interview, a team from the Journal showed up. The Journal photographer found more panhandlers and B-girls willing to pose.

At 2 a.m., the press, after buying me a drink, finally allowed me to grab a cab back to the Moreland.

Impassively, the night clerk handed me my key. He also handed me six telephone slips.

I studied the slips on the ride to the seventh floor. I had been asked to return calls to the Express, two television newsrooms, and the local bureaus of the Associated Press and United Press International. I had a suspicion those guys would keep calling all night.

The sixth slip reported a call from a "Ronald Layne, TA 4-5892." The word "Urgent" had been written across the face of the slip.

In the room, I hung up my coat, sat down, and dialed TA 4-5892. The bell sounded nine times before someone lifted the receiver.

"Who in hell is this?" a man asked.

"This is Kolchak. Stephen Kolchak."

"Christ, man. It's nearly dawn."

"Who are you? And what do you want with me?"

"Whatever it is, it can wait."

"You said it was urgent."

"Good grief. Look. I live at 429 Mason. That's a half block east of Clay at 1800 North. Why don't you drop around later today? Any time between noon and midnight."

Layne hung up.

I depressed the hook. I called the switchboard. I told the operator not to channel calls to me under any circumstances until ten o'clock.

Before turning in, I addressed another envelope to Max Fuller. In it, I placed a piece of paper on which I had printed, PHIL AMBER, GANG-STER.

CHAPTER 3

With the coming of the new day, the management of the Moreland Hotel began to appreciate my promotional possibilities. These were suggested by the growing stack of messages from communications media in my mailbox and the appearance, in the lobby, of men carrying cameras. My status began to change from that of unwanted guest to man of the hour. After all, whatever happened to my brother hadn't happened in the Moreland. It had happened far away on Clay Street. So what harm would come of insuring that all stories and television reports on me included mention of the Moreland? Where so many interesting visitors to the city liked to stay?

Thus at 9:30 a.m. the Moreland's manager paid a visit to my room. He bore a cellophane-wrapped basket of fruit. He also brought with him the girl who handled his public relations. She was sweet but crisp. Quickly she pointed out the advantages of holding a formal press conference and giving all the boys a break, instead of doling out interviews to a favored few, as I'd done at 1 a.m. on Clay Street. That way, all the boys would be on my side. It never paid to have any of the boys sore at you. I told her okay, you arrange everything, but I want it over in time to eat lunch and take off by three o'clock.

At eleven she called on the house phone and said, Come on down to the lobby, we're all set. A vote was taken when I arrived and it was almost unanimously decided to hold the conference in the cocktail lounge, away from the public's prying eyes. A television technician complained it would be hard setting up equipment in there, but he was overruled. He managed to set up his equipment anyhow.

I put on the performance expected of me. I figured I might as well make the most of my temporary notoriety. A week from now, I'd be last week's news. A month from now I'd be forgotten.

The Moreland supplied drinks all around. I hunched behind a table in a circular booth, my drink hidden on the seat. I stared intently at the television cameras and made a plea for anyone having any information whatsoever about my brother to come forward. I held up a huge enlargement of a photograph of my brother. One of the television men had conveniently supplied me with that. I clenched my fist and stuck my hand out and let the cameras focus on the ring. I described the watch, an ordinary cheap Time-0 on the outside, but with the name "Ed Kolchak" crudely scratched on the inside. My brother had scratched his name there himself with a penknife when he was ten years old, because he was so proud of that watch. My father had given it to him, and Ed had carried it ever since. Some men get sentimental over a commonplace item and never allow it out of their possession. Ed was that way about his pocket watch. It always kept perfect time. Ed liked to pull it out when time signals were given on the radio to compare it with the hands on his expensive wrist watch. Invariably, the wrist watch was maybe a half minute off.

As I completed my speech I had an inspiration. I announced I would offer a hundred-dollar reward for either the ring or the watch. I hoped the reward would serve to dramatize the importance of those articles.

The reporters threw me a lot of questions. I emphasized and re-emphasized my intention to remain in the city until I learned the truth. That was for the benefit of the unknown person or persons watching the television screen who knew the truth.

Some of the questions got rougher when the television boys packed up their film and turned off their recorders. Most of the newsmen were friendly and sympathetic. But one man—his name was George Nesbitt, and he was the chief crime beat man for the Journal—seemed determined to give me a hard time.

"Mr. Kolchak," he drawled, "do you have any idea why your brother never married?"

"I guess he never met the right girl."

"Did he live alone in Chicago? Or did he ever share an apartment with another man?"

"He lived alone."

"He was a good-looking boy, wasn't he. When he was a kid, did he ever form any special attachments with grown men? Schoolteachers, that sort of thing?"

I gazed with growing interest at Nesbitt, who was tall, thin, middle-aged, and already more than a little drunk.

"Yes. He was very close to his high-school football coach." Nesbitt's eyes lighted up. He began to phrase another question. I added, "The coach has five children and nine grandchildren, so far. Before taking up coaching, he played tackle eight years for the Chicago Cardinals."

For the moment, that stopped Nesbitt. But as the conference broke up and I elbowed through the lounge toward the lobby, Nesbitt tugged at my sleeve. He pulled me aside.

"Look, guy," he said. "Nothing personal. But when something like this happens, I cover all the angles."

"Sure."

"Let's face it. A lot of professional queers hang out on Clay Street. A lot of young guys go down there just for that. And your brother, a single kid with dough, where he wouldn't have to worry about anyone recognizing him."

"I understand."

"When you were small boys, did your brother ever like to dress up in his mother's clothes?"

I scratched my chin.

"Now that you mention it, I'll tell you something. Off the record." I took his arm. "Where these other guys won't hear."

I led him into the lobby and up a carpeted stairway. At the first turn, we were out of sight of both the lobby and the floor above.

I clenched my right fist and punched Nesbitt on the jaw.

The reporter bounced against the wall. He fell hard. He lay on his back, rubbing his jaw and snarling at me.

Without a word, I walked back down to the lobby. Two reporters collared me with more questions. Nesbitt came down a moment later. His face sported a big bruise. He glowered and made for the door. He passed a telephone booth in which the Associated Press man was hanging up.

The AP man looked at Nesbitt's face. He looked at me. He came over and shook my hand and said, "Nice going. If you hadn't done that, I think I would have."

After lunch I mailed Fuller a slip of paper on which I'd printed GEORGE NESBITT, JOURNAL CRIME REPORTER.

Sam Alban waited down the street in his cab. I piled in.

"Still going through with it?"

"You know it."

"Clay and Jackson?"

"No. Take me to 429 Mason."

I did not elaborate.

As he took off, Sam observed, "You're a real celebrity. I got the treatment too when your brother disappeared. But nothing like what you're getting."

"That won't last long."

"You're right," Sam agreed philosophically. "Four days after I took my lie test I coulda died and nobody would have cared."

Four-two-nine Mason was a three-story brick building with stone steps flanked by iron railings. In the vestibule I pushed the bell marked LAYNE. A buzzer sounded. I opened the vestibule door and started up.

On the first floor, a man waited. He was a squat youth, with upright and unkempt white hair and immense shoulders. He stood no more than 5'7" but weighed an easy 190. He wore khaki trousers, a T-shirt, and sneakers. A pug nose emerged from his round, hairless face. His mouth was small, his chin receding, his brow furrowed, and his eyes were pink.

"Whozzat?" he demanded.

"I'm Kolchak. Stephen Kolchak."

"Oh, the screwball." He turned and hollered into the apartment. "Hon, it's the three-ayem screwball I told you about."

"No kidding," a girl called out.

Layne stepped aside. I walked past him into chaos. The apartment was littered with books, magazines, newspapers, junk, ash trays, glasses, and glossy eight-by-ten photographs. Most of the photographs were of nearly naked young women. The exceptions were of entirely naked young women.

A small portable bar served as the room's focal point. A girl stood beside the bar. She couldn't have been a day over twenty. Her height was 5'1" at best. For a tiny thing, she was splendidly curved, a fact made even more obvious by her costume, an insignificant white bikini. She was barefoot. Her hair was dark and disheveled, her eyes wide and bright. Her nose was a pert button, her cheeks were red, and her strong little chin had a dimple on it.

"Betsy," Layne said, "this is Kolchak."

"Hi," Betsy said.

"Good afternoon." It was rude of me, but I couldn't help staring at her.

Layne closed the door.

"He likes you," Layne said to Betsy.

I looked away, for a place to sit down. There was no place to sit down. Junk covered the chairs and sofa.

Betsy grinned. She seemed pleased I liked her.

"Ronnie," she said, "why don't I fix coffee or something while you two talk business."

"Screw coffee. Make me the usual, you know how I like it. And bring the same for Kolchak."

Betsy wiggled to the kitchen. Casually, Layne knocked a pile of girlie magazines from a chair to the floor. He dumped a stack of photographs off another chair. With one brawny arm, he swept a jumble of empty film boxes from the sofa. He sat down on the sofa.

I sat down on a chair.

"You have a very attractive wife," I said.

Layne laughed. "She ain't my wife. She's a goddam model."

"You're a photographer?"

"Can't you tell?" He pointed to a door. "My studio's in there. I'm just getting started, see. So far I been specializing in cheesecake in between ratty little commercial jobs. You know. Layouts of girls from all angles."

"How did you know I was staying at the Moreland? And what do you want with me?"

"Well," Layne said, lighting a cigarette, "it was no trick finding you. It was all over the street that the Lost Man's brother was in town, going from one joint to another asking questions. And what's heard on the street, see, finds its way to me. As for finding you—I had a hunch you'd be at the Moreland. That's where your brother stayed. So I called and asked, and sure enough, that's where you were."

Betsy returned, a tall drink in each hand. She gave me mine and padded to Layne with his. Maybe Layne was accustomed to her near nudity at close quarters, but I wasn't. I raised the glass and took a deep swallow. I nearly gagged. I was drinking warm, cheap bourbon.

Betsy curled into the other cleared chair, her hands hugging her bare tummy.

"I think it's wonderful," she said. "I read about you in the paper this morning, Mr. Kolchak. I never had a little sister, but if I did and she got lost, I'd do the same thing. I'd go look for her no matter what."

"Thank you." I set the glass down. No more of that.

"I," Layne said, "have a proposition."

"What kind?"

"I want to shoot you. With the camera, of course."

"I've already been photographed. By guys from the newspapers."

"That's not what I meant." Layne leaned forward, smiling, his drink in hand. "I want to follow you around, see. On Clay Street. Everywhere you go. I'll be right beside you, working with fast film and miniatures. So I can use natural light. I'll get real arty stuff. Interiors and everything. Smoke-filled dives, strip joints, queers, the whole bit. A picture story about you looking for your brother on the street of lost men. It can't miss. You give me the exclusive right to shoot you, see, and after a week, I ought to have enough prints to sell a layout to Life, or Look, or the Saturday Evening Post. They'll pay a mint for a dramatic picture sequence like that. It'll be a real boost for me, too. It might get me some decent commercial jobs, so I won't have to mess around with this girlie crap. So I'll tell you what. We make this arrangement, see, and I'll pay you twenty-five percent of whatever I get."

For a moment I was too stunned to reply. Then I rose.

"No thanks."

Layne refused to believe me.

"Why not? What can you lose? You do what you'd do anyway, see. Only I'm there taking pictures of you doing it. You don't have to pay attention to me. You won't even hear the shutter click. And you'll rake in a couple hundred bucks at least."

"Sorry."

The photographer took a big swig from his drink.

"Awright. I'll make it fifty percent. And it's like you're stealing from my back pocket, because I'll be doing all the work, paying for the film and developer out of my share. But I'll do it for the prestige."

"Mr. Layne," I said slowly, "I came to this city for one reason only. To find my brother. Not to build your reputation or fatten your bank balance. The last thing I want is you or anyone else at my elbow, taking pictures of me and everyone I talk to. If this is what you made me come all the way up here for, I suggest you go back to your cheesecake and stay out of my path."

"It's a free country," Layne replied defensively. "If I want to follow you and shoot you anyhow, you can't stop me.

"You do that and I'll knock your block off."

"I can take care of myself."

He was right, too. Maybe I could lick him and maybe I couldn't. He had a slight edge in weight, he was all muscle, and he was maybe ten years younger.

"In addition to which," I said, "I'll tell my good friend Lieutenant Doyle at the Clay Street Precinct that you're hiding obscene photographs in here. His vice squad will put you under surveillance. They might even stage a raid."

It was an accurate stab in the dark. Given a man of Layne's unashamed greed, it stood to reason he'd earn a few extra dollars with pornography. The girlie prints strewn around the room came pretty close to pornography as it was.

"You don't scare me," Layne said. But his tone indicated I did.

"Mr. Kolchak," Betsy said, gazing up at me with wounded eyes, "I hope you don't think I'm that kind of a model."

I smiled. "Of course not. If I've offended you, I apologize."

I walked out, slamming the door behind me.

A little after 6 p.m., I watched myself on television.

I perched on a stool in a small cocktail lounge at 1613 North Clay, nursing a beer. The few other customers ignored me. I'd already questioned the bartender, who'd been civil but unenlightening.

Films and commentary on the Moreland press conference occupied much of the local telecast. I was shown holding up my brother's picture and displaying the ring. I described the watch. I offered the reward. I pleaded for anyone with information about my brother to contact me at the Moreland Hotel.

When the telecast ended, the bartender gazed at me in a thoughtful way. He came over with another bottle of beer.

"I didn't order that," I told him.

"That's all right. On the house."

"Well thanks."

I hadn't intended to drink another beer. But since he was the first bartender on Clay Street to do me a good turn, I refilled my glass.

"Tell you what," the bartender went on. "If you'd like to stick around in here all night, that'd be okay with me. You could have that table there. After the television show, when word gets around you're here, the joint will be packed with people wanting a look at you. You could question all of 'em. While you're doing it I'll give you anything you want to drink, free. I'll even send out for food. How about it? It will save you a lot of shoe leather."

The urge to bring the bottle down over the bartender's shiny skull was overpowering. But I resisted.

In a cafeteria across the street I got all the way through the food line before I was recognized. I found a back table. While I ate sausage and sauerkraut, people stared. More people came in and they stared too. I didn't enjoy eating with those eyes on me, but reflected that in a few days people would stop staring. I had sought publicity by holding a press conference and this was the price.

I was about to tackle dessert when Bill Totten, the Beacon reporter, and his photographer joined me.

"What's with you guys?" I asked. "The press conference is over."

"Follow-up," Totten explained genially. "A feature on your adventures tonight."

"How the hell do you expect me to accomplish anything with you hanging around?"

I said that in a jocular way, though. I'd expected further attention from the press for a while. But it would decrease quickly to nothing. And if I tried to avoid the press, the press would hound me anyway.

The photographer brought coffee for himself and the reporter. The three of us made small talk while I wolfed my pie.

As I pushed my plate back, a stooped old woman slipped through the tightly packed tables and stopped in front of us.

I'd seen her before, in one of the dives on the 1400 block. A black shawl covered her head. Over her shoulders she'd strapped a box of pencils. Apparently, she made her living selling pencils to sentimental drunks. I'd bought a pencil from her the night before, and asked her if she knew anything about my brother. She told me then she hadn't.

Now her bleary eyes viewed the reporter and the photographer with suspicion.

In a croaked voice she asked, "Who are they?"

"Friends of mine," I replied gently. "Don't be afraid. But I really don't need any more pencils."

She pulled up a chair. She sat down.

"It's not pencils, Mr. Kolchak. I've got your brother's watch."

I blinked. I said, "You do?"

"Yes."

"Where?"

"With me."

"Where did you get it?"

"I found it. In the alley, behind the mission, a long time ago. But I didn't open it up until tonight, after you talked about the watch on television. When I opened the watch, your brother's name was inside."

"Let me see it."

"Do you have the hundred dollars?"

"Not on my person. I don't carry that much money on Clay Street. I've only got about forty dollars in my pocket. But I could take you to the hotel and get it. Or write you a check."

"I don't want a check. You get the money and come back."

Totten cleared his throat. In an over-casual voice the reporter said, "I cashed my paycheck this afternoon. I could let you borrow the other sixty."

"There you are," I said. I hauled out my wallet and counted out forty-one dollars. Totten added fifty-nine. I put my hands over the pile. "Now let's see the watch."

The woman opened a purse and fumbled inside. She pulled out a watch. "See? The kind you said. A Time-O." With trembling hands and a bobby pin, she pried the back off. "Your brother's name is scratched in there." She held the watch up and waved it. The inside had been engraved all right. Quickly she closed the watch. "Here."

She slid the watch across the table and reached for the money. I grabbed her wrist.

"Just a minute." I turned to the reporter. "Open that again."

Totten opened the watch with a table knife. The name "Ed Kolchak" had been crudely scratched inside. But not by my brother. Even as a ten-year-old, Ed could print better than that. The watch was a fake.

"That's not my brother's watch," I said.

"His name's in it," she replied stubbornly. She put her wrinkled face up against mine. I smelled liquor and I didn't know what else.

I released her wrist. She pulled back.

"You keep the watch," I said. "I don't want it."

"You said on television you'd pay for it."

"But not that one. Only the real one."

"How was I to know that wasn't the real one? You ought to give me something for it. For my trouble. Five dollars, maybe. Or at least a dollar."

I said, "I'm not going to give you a cent. You tried to swindle me. I'm not going to reward swindlers on Clay Street or anywhere else."

She turned to the crowd. She shouted, "He won't pay! He said he'd pay and he won't pay! Not even a dollar! He won't pay!"

She was still hollering when the manager shoved her out the door.

I gave Totten his fifty-nine dollars back.

"Thanks," I said. "It's a nice world, isn't it. That telecast was less than an hour ago. Yet somehow that woman managed to get her hands on an old Time-0 watch and scratch my brother's name inside the lid."

"How much," the photographer asked, "did those old Time-0 watches cost?"

"Two dollars."

"And how many did they make?"

"I dunno. Millions, probably. Back then, you could buy 'em at every drug counter and dime store."

"You know," the reporter observed thoughtfully, "I got a hunch some more people might show up with engraved Time-0 watches. After all, you're offering a hundred-dollar reward for a two-dollar item. And all a guy has to do to qualify is scratch Ed Kolchak on the inside. I hope you got some other way to identify that watch, in addition to the engraving."

"I see what you mean," I said lamely.

"How about the ring? How much did that cost?"

"No problem there. It couldn't be reproduced in this country for less than a hundred."

But the reporter had a point. I recalled, in a general way, how Ed had scratched out that name. But any casual forger could probably come up by accident with a job reasonably similar enough to fool me. I hadn't seen the inside of that watch in four years.

BOOK TWO: JULY

CHAPTER 4

When I awoke, Lorene Heineman Powers stood beside my bed, bare arms folded over her chest. Her inscrutable blue eyes gazed into mine. Lorene and her father owned the building on Clay Street in which I now maintained an apartment. On the lower level, the Heinemans ran a restaurant called The Dugout. The apartment was the second I had occupied since leaving the Moreland in April, three months earlier.

How long Lorene had been standing there I did not know. Her white sleeveless blouse was smudged in places. Brown cotton pants, tapered snugly at her calves, encased the lower part of her body. A few beads of perspiration hung on her brow and in the cleft of her chin. Her pale blond hair, appealingly disarranged, stirred slightly in a warm breeze from the open window.

Lorene said, "Good morning. Or rather, good afternoon. It's twelve thirty."

I looked down. A sheet covered me. Moreover, I wore pajamas. I didn't recall going to bed. But if I had stopped to undress and don pajamas, I could not have been in too bad shape.

I looked back at Lorene.

"You," I said, "are one of the prettiest women I have ever viewed before breakfast, even if you are my landlady. Your nose is a little too long and has a slight bump on it. Your mouth is perhaps too wide. But for a thirtyish widow, you're remarkably well preserved."

Lorene was not amused.

"Aren't you curious," she asked, "about how I got in here?"

"I imagine you had a yen for me. And broke the door down."

Her low voice was curt. "I didn't have to break the door down. The door was open. You didn't close your front door last night. You must have been really loaded."

"It was that damn Harry Bagwell," I said. "He and some of his cronies were downstairs at the bar when I came in from my rounds. They asked me to have a drink with them. And one thing led to another."

"You don't have to drink with Harry Bagwell. Anyone who drinks with Harry Bagwell is courting delirium tremens."

I pulled the sheet aside. I swung my feet to the floor.

"I know. But the man fascinates me. Like a snake. Only he's more articulate."

Lorene moved toward the door. I loved to watch her move. Effortless. Covertly sensual. Like the slim, well-bred ladies she admired in fashion magazines.

"Hey, where are you going?"

"Down to the restaurant."

"Stick around. I'm just getting my strength back."

"I have work to do. I only came up here to be sure you were still alive. When you didn't show for coffee by noon and didn't even answer your doorbell, I thought I'd investigate. But I've seen men with hangovers before, so I think I'll leave now."

"What are you so sore about?"

"You. And what you could do to yourself. In your search for your brother."

"I don't get you. Will you be at the restaurant tonight?"

"No," Lorene said. "I'm going home where I belong. As far from Clay Street as I can get. To be with my son."

Despite the breeze, the day was hot. I showered. I knew very well why Lorene had been angry with me. Her anger had been inspired by her hatred of Clay Street. Lorene had been trying to get away from Clay Street all her life. The street's poverty dismayed her; its viciousness frightened her. But while she lived in a suburb now, she still worked on Clay Street.

I had experienced a touch of that anger the first time I saw Lorene, three weeks after I'd moved from the Moreland Hotel to a small apartment on Jackson. I had covered both sides of Clay ten blocks to the north of Jackson and had started south. I wore old clothes that day, since most of the signs to the south indicated workingmen's bars. I hadn't shaved. At four in the afternoon, I reached The Dugout.

To enter the restaurant you go down a short flight of stairs. After you pass the outer door you face two inner doors. One leads to the bar, the other to the dining room. Unknowingly, I picked the door to the dining area.

I found myself in a silent, screened foyer adjoining the cloakroom. The walls were decorated with World War I relics: a helmet, a gas mask, a doughboy's uniform in a glass case, campaign ribbons, and framed front pages with headlines about the Lusitania, the big battles, and the Armistice.

But what drew my attention was an oil painting, a portrait of a young woman. Illuminated by a recessed light at its base, the portrait hung under a bayoneted Enfield rifle. The woman's nose had a slight bump on it. Her face was long and somber; her mouth curved in the hint of a smile. She wore a French peasant girl's costume, the blouse cut almost to her nipples. The warm skin tones of her face, bare shoulders and arms, and the swell of her breasts shimmered in vivid contrast to the dark, murky background. Her eyes were wide and intense. Her expression was knowledgeable, inviting, and entirely serene. I thought her one of the most beautiful women I had ever viewed. In a moment of reverie, I forgot who I was, where I was, and what I was doing there.

A tray of glasses crashed to the floor.

I turned. I stared eye-to-eye with the woman depicted in the portrait. But a towel covered her hair; she wore pedal pushers and a sweat shirt. The tray lay at her feet.

"What," she asked unsteadily, "are you doing here?"

"It's a long story…"

"I know you," she went on, her composure returning, "and all like you. You must be new on Clay Street. Didn't they tell you? The Dugout is off-limits. It always has been, it always will be. This is a decent place. Clay Street bums don't come in here. So get out, before I call the police."

I began to say, "I'm looking for my brother…" Then I realized how boorish the statement would sound. I looked no different than what she had taken me for: an unshaven, poorly dressed Clay Street derelict. Venturing into her restaurant in old clothes had been a breach of good manners. If I'd taken the trouble to glance at the prices on the menu tacked to the front door, I'd have known better. Clay Street was like that. A few establishments designed for the rich thrived even near the heart of skid row.

"I'm sorry," I said. I left.

A few days later Lorene mailed me a note. She said one of her employees had told her who I was. My address had been easy to obtain. I'd stamped it on hundreds of ring designs I'd passed out. She invited me to return any afternoon. She signed the letter "Lorene (Mrs. Frank) Powers."

Before returning, I sent her name to Max Fuller. Max learned that Lorene had grown up on Clay Street in the apartment above the restaurant. Her father, John Heineman, had owned the building since 1925. During Prohibition he operated a profitable speakeasy there.

But the Depression impoverished Heineman's steady customers. By 1932, when Lorene was born, his savings had been wiped away. And most of the solid, middle-class citizens who formerly occupied the neighborhood began moving to the city's fringe, their place taken by the poor and dispossessed. Grimly, Heineman hung on. He rented half the downstairs space to a succession of small business enterprises. The other half, he decorated with his World War I memorabilia, to create a distinctive atmosphere and to fan memories of his own days in the A.E.F. He ran The Dugout primarily as a bar, with sandwiches for clerks and tradesmen on their lunch hours.

Heineman maintained a clean place. He kept the bums and sexual deviates out. But Lorene had to play and attend school in the neighborhood. She got to know the sights, sounds, and smells of Clay Street well. As a child, she helped her mother serve lunches in The Dugout. When she was older she took business courses at a free city college and enrolled in a correspondence school of restaurant management. Her dream was to build The Dugout into a first-class restaurant and sell it at a good price so her little family could buy another restaurant elsewhere.

Then Lorene met Frank Powers, a first lieutenant in the air force. Powers was twenty-eight, tall, slim, and handsome. An orphan, Powers had found in the service a dignity and purpose he had never enjoyed as a civilian. His future seemed assured, right on up to retirement at full pension. To Lorene, he offered his devotion and a chance to leave Clay Street forever. They were married within a month.

The Korean War had just ended. Powers, a navigator, was transferred from a nearby air base to Guam. Lorene followed. Her son, Jackie, was born in a naval hospital on the island. Lorene adapted easily to garrison routine. And after Guam, they might go to Germany, England, or a hundred other exciting places she'd never seen before. All of them a million miles from Clay Street.

Until one morning a plane carrying Powers and four other men took off on a routine patrol. It never returned. A few days later, a destroyer sighted floating wreckage and a life raft a hundred miles to the west.

There were no relatives on Powers' side. Lorene took Jackie back to Clay Street. For two years they lived above The Dugout. Lorene's mother had died. At first Lorene was too busy with the baby to give The Dugout much thought. But as time passed, her dream of developing a first-class restaurant took hold again. She added hot dishes to the noon menu. Clay Street's business and professional men soon learned that The Dugout served an excellent plate lunch for a dollar.

When Jackie was two, Lorene moved to a small apartment in a good residential area just off uptown. She didn't want the boy to roam Clay Street as she had. A neighbor helped watch the child. Lorene worked nights and weekends in swank uptown restaurants to learn more about restaurant operation. When Jackie was six, she enrolled him in a private day school. She bought an old car, so she could drive Jackie to school mornings and pick him up evenings.

Lorene had concluded that her original plan, to build up The Dugout alone and then sell it, would not work. The kind of restaurant she envisioned required an immense amount of money, much more than the government insurance on Powers' life, which she regarded as earmarked for Jackie anyhow. But if she and her father could get outside backing and the restaurant succeeded, their salaries and percentage of the profits would allow them to live comfortably while they saved for a restaurant all their own.

Lorene prepared a small dinner menu, a few entrees she made best, including some of her own invention. She hired a waitress and a part-time cook, a Puerto Rican boy named Tony. She priced the meals high, to discourage the wrong crowd. She served dinners only between six and eight-thirty or nine. Her purpose was not to make an immediate profit; it was to impress potential investors.

Lorene approached the local banks first. The bankers turned her down. Next she sought to induce some Clay Street merchants to form a syndicate. The merchants didn't have that kind of money. She sought out the backers of uptown restaurants where she'd worked, but those fellows couldn't have cared less.

Lorene kept plugging. She never got much of a dinner crowd, which was just as well: the old Dugout had space for only two dozen diners. Still, word of her excellent food spread. And one night a criminal lawyer and quasi-political figure named Harry Bagwell wandered in with two other middle-aged bachelors and a trio of call girls.

Bagwell dined on Lorene's specialty, hamburger stroganoff on wild rice. He asked for the chef. Lorene appeared. Bagwell demanded to know why she wasted her talents in such shoddy surroundings. Lorene said she and her father owned the restaurant. She told him about her late husband, her son, and her efforts to attract capital.

The next night, Bagwell returned with more friends; those friends brought wives. By week's end, a syndicate of seven investors had been formed, with Bagwell at its head. Lorene had the financing. The rest was up to her.

The Dugout was remodeled, with the bar in the original quarters and the dining room in what had been the adjoining store space. The bar was decorated as an immense shell hole, the dining room as a French cafe. The World War I relics were moved to the foyer. A shack south of the building was purchased and torn down to make a parking lot.

Bagwell insisted on the oil portrait of Lorene, which he paid for himself. An incurable lecher, he probably hoped the gesture would cause her to regard him as more than a business associate. But Lorene didn't let him touch her.

Lorene had thrown me out seven months after the grand reopening. When I went back, I was clean-shaven and wore a new suit. Lorene served me coffee. She said she recalled the night Ed disappeared because the police came around the next day. Business had been slow; Lorene, the waitress, and the cook had gone home early. John Heineman said he knew nothing about Ed either. Lorene invited me to stop at The Dugout any time I was nearby.

I returned often. Lorene was rarely present evenings now, when her father acted as host and greeter, but she was on hand every morning and afternoon. Without realizing it, I began telling her about myself—my boyhood, my days in the army, my life abroad. One night I caught the landlady at my Jackson Street apartment prowling my dresser drawers. She'd rented to me without knowing my identity; she had distrusted me ever since she learned it. I accused her of snooping and she charged that my presence frightened the other tenants. She ordered me out by the end of the week.

Lorene suggested I move into the apartment over the restaurant. She and her father had already moved to a house in the suburb; the boy, Jackie, would enroll in a suburban school that fall, away finally from Clay Street and the city. Heineman had planned to use the apartment on nights he remained later than usual, but he was driving home to the suburbs every night anyhow. They were already considering finding a tenant.

I accepted the offer. It would give me a Clay Street location where tipsters could reach me quickly. And I'd see more of Lorene.

After my shower, I dressed, walked downstairs, and opened the mailbox in the vestibule. I had received one letter. The envelope bore the imprint of the local chapter of the American Society of Engineers.

Upstairs I opened the envelope and found another report from Max Fuller. This one concerned a man named Martin Moss, who ran a schlock little advertising and public relations firm. Moss had just talked Lorene and her father into allowing him to handle advertising and promotion for the restaurant.

I'd met Moss in the restaurant a few nights previously. However, I'd spoken to him on the telephone once back in April when I was still living at the Moreland. Moss called and offered to plant me on some local television shows to spread my story. In exchange, he said, all I had to do was mention on the air that I could be reached every night the remainder of that week in Booth No. 4 of a certain night club, by no coincidence a Moss client. The booth would be reserved for me and so long as I occupied it, I would not have to pay for a thing.

My response had been to hang up. But since Martin Moss had now intruded upon my life a second time, an investigation seemed in order.

Fuller said Moss, thirty-five, was married and the father of four children. He lived six blocks east of Clay and maintained a small office a block west of Clay. His neighbors regarded him as a devoted husband and parent. Moss grew up in the Clay Street area. Until drafted in 1951, he sold advertising for a community newspaper. He served with no particular distinction in Korea and then obtained a minor job with a small advertising agency. After a while he picked up so many accounts on the side that he went into business on his own. His clients, most of them from Clay Street, included four night clubs, two restaurants, a savings and loan, a bank, a merchant's association, and a pizzeria. Phil Amber owned one of the restaurants and two of the clubs.

I dropped the Moss report into a box with the others. In fourteen weeks I'd collected reports on about thirty people, ranging from Doyle, Betsy, and Ronnie Layne to Lorene, her father, and Harry Bagwell. On dull nights, the reports made dull reading.

Downstairs in the restaurant, Lorene's father brought me coffee and a roll at the bar. I took it there because the dining room was still filled with the tail end of the luncheon crowd. Lorene's father put the cup down and asked, "What did you say to Lorene just now? She's mad as hell."

"It'll pass. She was upset about last night."

"You did overdo, you know." John Heineman was a large man. He stood maybe 6'1" and weighed about 240. His hair was close-cropped, his face square, ruddy, and open. His big nose had a bump on it like Lorene's. His brows were thick and blond, like his hair. His eyes were gray, his lips full. "When you got up at closing time, I had to point the way to the door."

"It was Bagwell. Dammit, he kept shoving drinks into my hand, all the while trying to bait me into an argument. I'd have been okay if I'd eaten a decent dinner. But all I had was a sandwich around eight o'clock."

Heineman forced himself to smile. I sensed he really didn't like my presence in the apartment upstairs, that he was being polite to me for Lorene's sake. "Don't take Bag-well too seriously. He's not the most pleasant guy in the world when he's drinking. But as a lawyer, he's helped a lot of people in trouble."

"He also represents the underworld. Whenever a hoodlum is arrested, Harry shows up at the station house with a writ."

"Look at it this way. He uses that money to defend someone like that colored boy. The one those suburban cops were railroading on a fake assault charge. Or the old Polish lady who poisoned her husband…"

"But with what tactics? He was nearly disbarred three times. Once for a wiretap scandal, when he and some politicians put a tap on a district attorney. And twice for bribing jurors…"

"He was a marine in the war," Heineman replied defensively. "At Iwo, he won a medal."

That, to Heineman, ended the argument. Anyone who had won a medal could do no wrong. Scowling, the old soldier wandered away to draw a beer. For a man of sixty, he moved with amazing ease. It must have been a family trait. Fuller had noted that Heineman suffered from a mild cardiac condition. It didn't seem to have slowed Heineman down much. Lorene's father arrived for work before noon every day and stayed until 2 a.m.

From a booth in The Dugout, I telephoned the Moreland Hotel. The desk switched me to the doorman. I told the doorman to ask Sam Alban to pick me up at the restaurant. Ordinarily, Sam cruised the uptown area near the Moreland. Since he rarely got a fare to Clay Street, we used the Moreland doorman to shuttle my messages. Sam would get into the Moreland cab line whenever he was in that block, every hour or so. If I wanted a ride, the doorman would tell Sam, and Sam would come get me. I offered to pay the doorman for his trouble, but he refused to accept my money. I guess he had a brother of his own.

Sam picked me up at half past two.

He asked, "Where we headed?"

"First, the convention hall. Betsy wants to see me. Then we'll run out to the bakery."

Sam pulled the cab into traffic. "Gonna hit the street again tonight?"

"Sure. I'm down to the seven-hundred block for the second time. Flop-house row."

"Anything new?"

"No. But I had that feeling again. As though someone was following me. I thought I glimpsed the guy about a block behind me as I was walking back to my apartment. So I stopped at the bar downstairs to see who'd come in after me. Nobody came in. While I was watching, Harry Bagwell and some of his friends lured me into their booth. After that, I don't remember much."

"Maybe it was another of Doyle's detectives."

"I doubt it. They never tried to hide. And they haven't dogged me for nearly two months."

"What do you think?"

"I'm hoping," I said grimly, "this is the nibble I've been waiting for. And if it is, someone may make a move before long."

CHAPTER 5

The municipal convention hall, a huge, new, oblong structure, occupied a landscaped block near the business district. The state bankers' association was meeting there. Betsy had arranged for my admittance to a trade show being held in conjunction with the convention.

I found the little model in front of Booth 94, garbed in a wide-skirted, white fairy queen outfit. She was handing ball-point pens to passers-by. The pens were imprinted with the name of a distributor of office machines, the firm that had engaged her from the modeling agency. Inside the booth, a lean, crew-cut boy in a one-button gray suit lounged in a chair amidst rows of gleaming tabulators, waiting for a strolling banker to express interest in the merchandise.

When Betsy saw me, she grinned. She waved a fistful of pens.

"Hi, Steve. You bring 'em?"

"I brought 'em."

"Then gimme."

She led me into the booth. The young man had been staring at Betsy with curiously vacant eyes. Now he roused himself and paid attention to me.

"This is Don," Betsy explained. Don rose. We shook hands. "Don, this is the man I was telling you about. Steve Kolchak."

"I saw you on television once." Don's voice had the genial, confident ring of a well-born and prematurely successful youth. He was twenty-five at most.

"Don," Betsy added, "is a vice-president of his company."

"You've done well," I observed, "for a man your age."

"That's because I'm the best salesman M. J. Collins, Inc., ever hired," Don replied casually. "The fact that my father happens to be M. J. Collins has absolutely nothing to do with it."

Betsy said, "Steve brought me more copies of the design on the ring his brother was wearing."

I hauled the sketches from my jacket pocket. Betsy took them.

"Betsy," I said to Don, "is my cavalry. She charges all over town with these."

"Excuse me," Betsy said. "I promised some to that nice boy in Booth 48. He's going to distribute them to bank tellers."

Betsy skipped away.

"She sure thinks a lot of you," Don said, a little enviously.

"Betsy feels sorry for me, that's all. She's still a little girl who brings home lost kittens and birds with busted wings. But I can't turn down the kind of help she's offered. She's got every model in her agency showing those sketches around."

'You're lucky. She's not just another cute model. She has real character. And she's a lot smarter than most people think."

"How long have you known her?"

"I first met Betsy," Don Collins said, "about an hour ago." Traffic at the trade show was light. When Betsy returned, we chatted awhile. I didn't think it my place to tell Collins how I'd first met Betsy, in Ronald Layne's cluttered studio apartment a half block from Clay Street. Nor did I tell him how Betsy had telephoned me at the Moreland a few days later to thank me for, as she put it, "exposing" Ronald Layne. My crack to Layne about pornographic pictures, and Layne's reaction, had disturbed her. So while putting her clothes on in Layne's studio dressing room, she conducted a search and found a bundle of pornography in a carton behind a screen. That so angered her that on the way out, without a word, she slapped the photographers face. She also quit the agency that had sent her to Layne and landed a job with another one. During our phone conversation she offered to enlist her roommates and other friends in the search for my brother's ring. Thus I took Betsy to lunch one day and inducted her into my army.

Max Fuller's report on Betsy Ryan disclosed that she'd grown up in a small town near the state capital. Her mother was a waitress, deserted by Betsy's father when Betsy was still an infant. Betsy's mother died shortly after Betsy finished high school. Betsy came to the city with the pittance remaining of her mother's insurance money. She used her inheritance to enroll at a modeling school. She lived with two other models in an apartment approximately two miles from Clay Street.

Don Collins expressed polite interest in my search. He asked some innocuous questions. Then his eyes strayed down the aisle. "Excuse me. But here comes a very live customer."

"Sam's outside with the meter running," I said. "I'd better get back before it explodes."

Betsy reached for her ball-point pens. "What are you working on now, Steve?"

"I'm going to have another talk," I said, "with the people who found my brother's watch."

Sam pulled up in front of Bronson's Bakery. The real watch had turned up here, seven miles from the intersection of Jackson and Clay. The neighborhood was old. Frame homes and brick walk-up apartment buildings lined its quiet streets. The bakery itself was on a block of dusty little stores and shops. Several store fronts were vacant. The few pedestrians in view—an old man, a woman pushing a perambulator, two subteens in shorts—gave eloquent testimony as to why. Business could hardly be deader.

I had no doubt as to the watch's authenticity. The baker's daughter, Irma Bronson, had found the watch when sweeping the floor one evening. That had been seven months after my brother disappeared, five months before I came to the city. The watch lay under a radiator near the front door. Apparently it had fallen from someone's pocket.

The watch had stopped. The baker, Kurt Bronson, opened it to assess the damage. He noted the name "ED KOLCHAK" scratched crudely inside. He shook the watch; it began to tick again. Once more, it was keeping perfect time.

The baker and his daughter posted a sign on their counter. The sign said: FOUND – TIME-O POCKET WATCH, OWNER MAY HAVE BY IDENTIFYING NAME INSIDE CASE. No claimant came forward. After a few weeks, the baker took the sign down. He dumped the watch into a drawer and forgot it. Until, four months later, he heard and saw me describe the watch on his television screen.

Bronson didn't call me immediately. He delayed one day. He didn't want to get mixed up in a police investigation. But Irma nagged at his conscience and finally induced the baker to dial the Moreland. By then I was dubious of anyone claiming to have found Ed's watch. I had examined and rejected five fake watches so far. For future claimants, I had memorized a little speech.

"I'm grateful for your information," I told Bronson. "I hope you won't mind. But before I pay the reward, I'd like you to take a polygraph test, at your convenience and at my expense. You'll be asked only one question. Specifically, did you or anyone you know scratch my brother's name in that watch?"

"You've got some nerve!" Bronson hollered. "We found the watch months ago. And I can produce at least fifty people who'll remember seeing the sign I put up seeking the owner!"

Just barely, I persuaded Bronson not to hang up before giving me his name. The lie test proved unnecessary. One look, and I knew the watch had been Ed's. I noted a slight chip on the crystal. I recalled that I'd put it there myself when I accidentally knocked the watch off a table. Kurt Bronson got his hundred dollars. But although payment of the reward was covered in the newspapers, three more people tried to sell me watches during the remainder of the week.

I walked into the bakery. A bell tinkled. Irma Bronson came out to wait on me. A blond woman, she was buxom and tall. Her eyes were large and blue. Her nose was straight, cast in a classic Grecian mold. Her lips were full, and her jaw was strong. She looked a year or so older than the twenty-nine noted by Max Fuller. As befitting a baker's daughter, she was garbed in a white apron.

I said, "Hi, Irma. Your father back there?"

"He is."

"I'd like to talk to him. And you, too."

"Mr. Kolchak, I don't understand. We told you everything last April."

"I know. But I've had a new thought. And I'd like to discuss it with both of you."

Irma led me into the back. Under the apron, her buttocks moved rhythmically. Her beam was broad and her legs were thick, but if she ever married a man who could keep her away from the bakery, Irma might slim down into quite a woman.

Bronson was rolling dough. He frowned.

"What do you want this time?"

"Can we be alone a minute? You, me, and Irma?"

Bronson turned to a Puerto Rican boy helping him. "Go out front," he ordered. "Take care of customers. And remember, I can tell to the penny what should be in the register."

A nice, trusting guy, Bronson. The three of us climbed a stairway to his apartment. Bronson eased into a big chair. He was tall, bald, and very fat. Irma settled demurely on a sofa, hands clasped on her ample lap. I pulled up an uncomfortable straight-backed chair.

"Well, what is it?" Bronson demanded. "We've already seen you a half-dozen times. And that Lieutenant Doyle, he comes around every other week. It's like we said. The watch was on the floor. We don't know who dropped it. What else is there?"

"I have a request to make."

"Such as?"

I lit a cigarette. I avoided Kurt Bronson's wary eyes.

"Well, you know the situation. The watch could have been dropped by a salesman or by a supplier making a delivery. But the odds are nine in ten it was dropped by a customer. And as you told me and the police, most of your customers are people who come in here more than once. People from this neighborhood."

"Sure. But except for a few, we don't know their names. Irma waits on most of the people, she might recognize their faces, but who they are and where they live, we don't know."

"Exactly. It isn't a certainty. Some stranger could have walked in here, bought something, and dropped the watch. But the chances are very high the watch was dropped by a fairly regular customer. Possibly someone who still patronizes your bakery. And so I got an idea. I thought: Why not bring

Irma down to Clay Street? To Clay and Jackson. And have her look at the people who pass that intersection. She might recognize one of your customers.

Bronson's round face turned red.

"That's crazy. Anyone could have dropped that watch. A man driving by in a car who decided he wanted a loaf of bread. A repairman. Anybody. It's nice you gave us the hundred dollars for finding the watch. But we don't want to get involved any more. What happened to your brother, it's not our concern."

I looked at Irma.

"It's your daughter's decision, Mr. Bronson."

"I think," Irma said uncertainly, "like my father thinks."

"I won't stand for it," Bronson went on. "My daughter down on Clay Street. Who knows who lives on Clay Street? You should know, by now. Drunkards. Degenerates. Morons and worse, yet. That's where you want my daughter to go? My Irma grew up in a respectable home. One day, she'll have a respectable husband. Her mother, rest her soul, if she knew this, she'd throw you out. My Irma is a good girl."

"Shell be safe. I'll rent an office overlooking Clay and Jackson. All Irma has to do is look out the window at the people walking by. And tell me whenever she recognizes someone."

"No police, even?"

"I'd rather do this without their knowledge. If the police were involved, word might get out and the whole project would be ruined."

"You're a madman."

I rose. I jammed my hands into my pockets. Staring hard at Irma, I said: "Look. For three months I've been getting nowhere down there. I've talked to everyone who'd talk to me. Night after night. And that isn't all. I bought back copies of every edition of every newspaper printed in this town within a week either way of my brother's disappearance. I checked out every story that could conceivably have even the remotest possible connection. Obituaries, accidents, crimes. I've had doors slammed in my face, telephones banged in my ear. And you represent the only lead left now to what happened to my brother. If we find one of your regular customers has business that takes him to Clay and Jackson, we may be able to solve the case in ten minutes. All I ask is that you think it over. And give me your answer later."

Irma looked at the floor.

Kurt Bronson said, "All right. I'll think it over. I'll give it every consideration. But I can tell you right now, my answer is no."

Sam drove me back to my apartment. The entrance was private, at 1019 North Clay, adjoining the restaurant entrance at 1015 Clay. I fixed myself a supper of canned beans and wieners. I changed to old clothes and set out on my evening rounds. But I was still fatigued from my drinking bout with Bagwell. I returned home early, a little after ten.

An envelope jutted from my mailbox. I extracted it. The envelope bore no return address and had not been postmarked. My name was printed on its face in pencil.

Upstairs I found two items in the envelope.

One was a printed note. It said:

> HERE'S PROOF WE KNOW ABOUT YOUR BROTHER. IF YOU WANT TO KNOW, GET TWO THOUSAND DOLLARS CASH. BE AT THE CAVE ON 18TH STREET AT 8 TOMOR-ROW NIGHT. WE'LL WATCH. ANY COPS OR REPORTERS AND NO DEAL.

The other item was the top portion of a credit card that had been cut in two. The name on the card was "Edmund L. Kolchak." I checked the card's number against a list given to me by the Chicago police department. The numbers corresponded. The card was genuine. It was one of the credit cards my brother had on his person when he disappeared.

In the morning I rode a bus uptown. I got off near the business district. In a drugstore I entered a telephone booth and dialed Max Fuller's office. I had not talked to the old private detective since my first day in the city.

Fuller's office did not answer. I tried the unlisted home number.

An elderly woman said, "Hello?"

"This is Mr. Kay. I'd like to speak to Max."

"Max is on a job now. But I'll reach him. What's your number there?"

I read off the number of the booth phone.

"Hang up and stand by. He won't be long."

I stepped outside the booth and lit a cigarette. I was half through it when the telephone rang.

I hopped back in.

"Max?"

"Yes, Mr. Kay." The deep voice was calm and unhurried. "We have an emergency?"

"We do. I received a note offering to sell information about my brother for two thousand dollars. I'm to make contact with the informant in a bar on Eighteenth Street. The note is crude, but the author must know something. He enclosed a portion of one of the credit cards my brother carried in his wallet."

"What action did you have in mind?"

"I want to borrow two thousand dollars from you. In cash, and in small bills. I need the money today. I have a good deal more than that in the bank, but if I make a withdrawal of that size, I'm afraid Doyle and the police might hear of it. The bank is on Clay Street."

"Very well. I'll arrange the loan. Anything else?"

"No. I'll handle the rest. Finding that watch hasn't been much help so far. This could be the first real break in three months. I don't want any cops or private eyes or anyone else queering this deal."

"It's your decision. Personally, I'd advise getting all the help you can. Doyle knows how to handle these things. But you're a stubborn cuss, I don't suppose I can change your mind."

"You can't."

"In that case, follow this procedure. At eleven this morning, enter a men's shoe store at 583 East Washington. The manager is one of my nephews, he'll wait on you. Buy a pair of shoes. Tell him you'd like to make payment with a check, but you forgot your checkbook. He'll take the shoes away to wrap them. But the package he brings back will contain the money. Two thousand should go into a shoe box nicely. My nephew will give you a document to sign. Only it won't be a check. It'll be your note to me, for the two thousand. That's so I can collect from your estate in the event something unfortunate happens to you before you can make repayment."

A little before noon I opened the package in my apartment and counted the money. I rewrapped it and put it on a closet shelf, on top of a stack of photographs of Betsy Ryan. To be sociable, I had once asked Betsy to give me some of her modeling prints. Betsy had obliged with a bundle, from cheesecake to high fashion.

I opened a drawer and pulled out a small case containing my gun, a .38 Colt Bankers Special. I'd bought it and a shoulder holster years ago from an oil refinery security chief, after a pair of thugs knifed me in Tangiers while stealing the equivalent of four dollars American from my person. I'd worn the gun a few times since but had never fired it in anger.

Carefully I cleaned and oiled the gun. I slipped it into the holster and put it back in the drawer. I'd load it later, when I was ready to go.

Attired in a demure gray dress, Lorene met me as I walked into the restaurant for lunch. She carried a few menus in one hand and her smile was automatic and professional. But at least, no spark of hostility flared in her eyes. She led me to a corner table.

"Care for a cocktail?"

"I think not."

"The goulash is very good today. Besides, hardly anyone is ordering it. Were going to have a lot left over. Like the chop suey last Tuesday."

That, for the time being, signaled the end of the war.

I said, "I'll have goulash. Tomato juice. French dressing on the salad. A pot of tea. And maybe later, conversation with you."

"I'll give your order," Lorene said, "to the waitress."

After I finished my meal, Lorene rejoined me. The dining room had nearly emptied. It was nearly two.

"Good grief," Lorene sighed. "How'd you like another five pounds of goulash? I can let you have it cheap."

"You can't win 'em all."

"I guess not. Stephen—I'm sorry about yesterday."

"Don't apologize. It was the nicest awakening I've ever had."

"I had no business barging into your apartment. I should have closed your door and walked back down here. And I have no right to pass any judgments on you. It's just that—well, you know how I feel about Clay Street."

"I don't mind. I like your taking an interest in an ugly lug like me."

"You're not ugly."

"The hell I'm not. I've got a face like a thug in a Grade-B movie. You know what they called me in high school? 'Monk.' That's because I resemble a goddamned ape. The only girls who look twice at me are homely old maids willing to settle for anything."

"I'll look twice at you."

"Then why don't you let me get you away from this restaurant sometime? Maybe you, me, and Jackie. I've never met your son. Why don't we take him to the zoo?"

Slowly Lorene said, "You know how I feel about that."

"I can't stop, Lorene. I have to find Ed. Or learn what happened."

"I know that too. I don't want you to stop. But so long as you're devoting all your time to your search, you're not a normal man. You're a man with a mission that's more important to you than anything else. And before I bring any man friend home to meet Jackie, that man is going to be leading a normal life, like other people. Not spending all his waking hours looking for a brother on Clay Street." Lorene smiled. "Besides, if I knew you better, I might not like you, and you might not like me. Remember, I'm not promising anything. Anyhow, when you learn what happened to your brother, you may decide you'd be better off with someone like the little model you bring around once in a while."

"Betsy? She's just a child."

"The way she looks at you," Lorene said, "I think she entertains some grown-up notions."

CHAPTER 6

I had intended to go upstairs after lunch. But as I started for the door, a man seated alone in a corner pushed his chair back and rose.

"Mr. Kolchak," he said. I'd like to talk to you."

I had seen the man during the lunch hour before. He seemed to know Lorene, since she stopped at his table sometimes to chat. The man was about my age and height, but considerably trimmer. He wore a rumpled brown suit. His straight blond hair needed combing. Thick, rimless glasses shielded his eyes. His face was squarish and determined. For my benefit, he tried to affect an expression of cordiality, but it was obvious he had something on his mind and didn't want to waste time.

"I'm Pete Ordway," he added, extending a hand. We shook. "Maybe you've noticed my shingle down the street. At 939 Clay."

Indeed I had. The sign identified Peter J. Ordway as an attorney-at-law. It hung from a second-floor office above a string of stores and shops. Like Ordway, the sign struck me as a trifle seedy.

"Shall we talk here?"

"Let's go to my office. You might say this is business."

Ordway had already paid his check. Apparently he had been waiting for me to leave. We strolled outside. The air was warm and muggy. A bank of gray clouds was moving in from the west. Clay Street lay brooding under a smoky haze.

"How's your search going?"

"Nothing new," I replied noncommittally. "But I'm a patient man."

"That," Ordway said, "is what we thought."

We turned into Ordway's building and hiked up a flight of stairs. Ordway's secretary, a middle-aged woman, threw him a mechanical smile. Ordway led me to an inner office. He closed the door.

If Ordway was a success as a lawyer, it didn't show in his furnishings which looked secondhand. I walked to a window and peered out.

"You have a nice view of Clay Street," I observed. "You weren't by any chance working late the night my brother disappeared, were you?"

"Sorry." Ordway sat behind his desk. "I do hang around late sometimes. Most of my clients work days and can't afford to take time off. But that night, my wife had to help my father at the store. It's the pharmacy at the corner—Clay Drugs. The regular cashier took sick. So I went home early to keep the baby in fresh diapers."

I recalled visiting the drugstore. I'd talked to an elderly man there.

I sat down and lit a cigarette.

Ordway said, "Kolchak, I won't screw around. Me and some friends of mine, we want to exploit you."

"Well, that's a novelty." I chuckled. "The exploitation idea. When I was front-page news a few months ago, every opportunist in town was trying to cash in on my name. But your candor, at least, is a refreshing change."

"I can imagine. Here's my angle. My dad is one of the old-timers around here. Just as Lorene's father is. I grew up on this block. Lorene went steady with me, in fact, during my senior year in high school. She was a sophomore. But I'm not like Lorene. All she's ever wanted to do was to run away."

"I know."

"Me, I plan to stick it out. Not that I think anyone will ever work a miracle and bring back the good old days. But a lot of decent people still live around Clay Street—old residents like my dad, and new residents whose only crime is they're poor and ignorant. At the very least, they deserve a fair shake from City Hall. But they're not getting it. Hiram Schell is ward committeeman for the majority party, the mayor's party. Schell has an alliance with Phil Amber. Schell picks the police captain for the Clay Street Precinct. That's because the city still uses the district system. Each district police commander rules his own empire. The system is tailor-made for political interference. As a result, the cops down here are more concerned with preserving order in Amber's joints than with helping people who need help. Schell's influence with the mayor stems from the fact he can deliver this ward with fantastic majorities every election day. And in addition to keeping Clay Street wide open, Schell blocks all proposals for urban renewal in this ward. Amber is afraid that might not be good for business. Even so, we could beat the Amber-Schell alliance if the ward had one dominant minority group that would vote in a block against them. But as it is, our ward is a mixture of old white residents, Mexicans, Negroes, Puerto Ricans, hill people, and some Bohemians and intellectuals. Everybody hates everybody else. Schell plays one group off against the other and then bribes influentials in each group to become his precinct captains."

"What's all this got to do with me?"

"There's an election in November. We think you can help us."

"You're out to capture the ward from Hiram Schell?"

"Christ, no. We could never oust Schell's alderman from this ward. Schell's organization will fall apart when he dies. But so long as he's alive, he's got this ward all locked up. The group I'm with—we're out to clobber the mayor."

Ordway guessed at the question forming in my mind. He glanced around his shabby office and permitted himself a faint smile.

"I'm sorry I can't make my proposition in more impressive surroundings. I just passed the bar a year or so ago. I had to help my father with the drugstore days and attend law school nights. That took me longer than most because I'm not such a hot student and I had to quit for a while when my wife was sick. But when I was in law school, one of my instructors, a man with a nice corporate practice uptown, got me a job as a part-time investigator for the Clean Government League. You familiar with it?"

"No"

"Well, it's what the newspapers call a watchdog' group. It's privately supported by contributions from merchants and businessmen. The CGL checks to see that tax money is spent the way it's supposed to be spent. That's what merchants and businessmen are mainly after—lower taxes. The CGL sends snoopers to follow city work crews around to see if they do a day's work for a day's pay, all that crap. They send representatives to howl at every public budget hearing. But recently the CGL has developed an interest in the influence of Syndicate crime on City Hall. Specifically, Phil Amber's influence on the mayor, through Hiram Schell. The CGL hired me to hang around Amber's joints, note any flagrant law violations and report 'em. Then the CGL would make the reports public and demand to know why the police weren't enforcing the law."

"I can't say," I observed, "your reports seem to have done much good."

"We really didn't expect 'em to. Mainly, we were giving the mayor a message. Letting him know the business community in this city is fed up with Clay Street's running wide open. There are still some big businessmen here who want a wide-open strip—they say it's good for drawing conventions and so on. But the majority has decided a thorough cleanup on Clay Street is long overdue. They also want to tear down a portion of this neighborhood for urban renewal and condemn a big strip for an east-west expressway. Through the mayor, Schell is blocking all that. But if the mayor and his party lose in November, Schell won't be able to block it any more. Schell won't be able to name the district police captain, either. The opposition candidate has pledged to bring in a new police commissioner, end the district system, and reorganize the force into a modern, centralized department. After which a cleanup of Clay Street will be one of the first orders of business."

"You think you can beat the mayor?"

Ordway pulled a pipe from his pocket. Thoughtfully he lit it. "For the first time in years, the minority party has a fighting chance. The candidate couldn't be better. He's a young, self-made industrialist with a national reputation. His firm never had any labor trouble. He has a solid war record, a wife, and four children. He's a persuasive speaker and he looks good on television. More important, he and his friends—people like the directors of the CGL—have passed the hat and come up with a whopping big campaign fund. Were going all-out this time, building organizations in every ward where the mayor's party doesn't have a stranglehold. And when the campaign gets under way, we're going to hit hard on Clay Street and the Syndicate crime issue."

I stubbed the cigarette out. Ordway's political science lecture had been enlightening, but I was anxious to get back to my apartment. In a few hours, by paying someone two thousand dollars, I might finally learn what had happened to my brother.

"Exactly what is your proposition?"

"I'm retained on the CGL's legal staff now," Ordway said, "and while the CGL itself is nonpartisan supposedly, most of our directors are backing the minority candidate for mayor. I'm very close to the people running the campaign. Our plan is to put conditions on Clay Street under a constant glare of publicity from the middle of September right up through election day. The publisher of the Beacon and its sister paper, the Express, will give us full cooperation. The Journal doesn't like us much, but they won't be able to ignore us either."

"The press," I said, "doesn't care about me any more. I'm old stuff. I could stand on my head at Clay and Jackson and I wouldn't get a line."

"That's true now," Ordway replied. "But it might not be true if you learned what happened to your brother between now and October. And our proposition assumes that you will have found your brother by then—or will have decided to quit your search entirely. We realize that your search for your brother is your main consideration. If you're still looking for him in October, we won't hamper you by trying to involve you in a political campaign."

"All right. Suppose I do find Ed. Tomorrow, next week, or next month."

"In that case, we'd like you to consider sitting down with a team of reporters from the Beacon. The publisher is a CGL director and he's assured me he'll go along. We're not asking that you give the Beacon an exclusive story on how you found your brother, or looked for him. All we're asking is that you tell those reporters what you've seen on Clay Street—the wide-open vice, the poverty, the misery, everything. Tell it honestly—every rotten sight, sound, and smell. Then the Beacon will print a series of front-page articles in October giving your impressions of conditions in Hiram Schell's ward."

I shook my head. "I think you're nuts."

"Oh, we don't think your articles will win the election for us. But a series by you, running in the Beacon at the same time we hit Schell and the mayor with our other material, would be a big help."

"You're asking quite a bit from me. What would I get in return?"

"First, the knowledge that you were doing the right thing. Second, I won't insult you by pointing out that the Beacon will pay you for the articles. And third, were offering all the help we can give in your search. Let me emphasize also that were not asking that you agree now to write the articles. We ask only that you agree to take our request seriously. If and when you find your brother, then you can make your final decision."

"How can the CGL help me find Ed?"

"Admittedly there's not much we can do. But the CGL's people do circulate around town quite a bit. I understand you're looking for your brother's ring. If you could give me some copies of the design, I could circulate them to every CGL investigator. They might be able to pick up something."

It was a thought. A whole new troop of cavalry in my army.

"What's more, our directors are men of considerable influence. Circumstances could arise where you'd want influence on your side, if you follow me."

"I do. Ordway, give me a few days to sleep on this."

"Certainly."

I rose. "By the way, it's probably a good thing Phil Amber never learned you were snooping in his clip joints for the CGL. That could be dangerous work."

"Oh, Amber found out about it," Ordway said casually. "He learns everything. Of course at the time I thought I had him by the balls. If he did anything to me then, the newspapers would have murdered him, and Clay Street, too. I told him that to his face and he took it. But a year later—after I left the CGL to cram for the bar exam—a street gang caught me and my wife when we were walking home late from the drugstore. Teenagers. They fractured my skull and broke three of my ribs. My wife, they broke her arm and were dragging her by the ankles into an alley when, thank God, a squad car rounded the corner. I could never prove it, but I know Phil Amber arranged it. The next morning, for the first time in his life, Phil Amber walked into my fathers drugstore. He bought a stick of gum with a dollar bill, told my father to keep the change, and walked out laughing. That, Mr. Kolchak, is the kind of man Phil Amber is."

I rode a bus to The Cave, a tavern several miles from Clay Street in a workingman's neighborhood where it was unlikely I would be recognized. I carried the shoe box under my arm. Despite the muggy heat, I wore a faded sports jacket to cover the shoulder holster.

I was the only passenger off at the 18th Street intersection. I watched the bus rumble away. I turned around and walked four doors to the tavern, which was adjoined on one side by a Polish delicatessen and on the other by a real-estate office owned by two Bohemians. My stomach was hollow and acid. I'd planned to nap and then grab a quick supper in my apartment, but I'd been too nervous to either sleep or eat.

The Cave's interior was packed. No doubt most of the patrons worked in the row of factories stretching for blocks in both directions on the south side of 18th Street. I elbowed to the end of the stand-up bar and ordered a glass of beer. It was 7:52 p.m. The bartender didn't give me a second glance. I sipped and waited, listening to a babble of voices and the blare of a television set.

At 8 p.m. precisely, during a commercial for "Route 66," a telephone rang in a corner booth. A man seated at a table nearby got up and answered it. He stuck his head out the booth and hollered, "Anybody here named Kolchak?"

I set the beer down and pushed through the mob. "That's me."

The man shrugged and returned to his table. My name seemed of no apparent interest to anyone. I slipped into the booth and closed the door. I rested the shoe box on the shelf and reached for the dangling earpiece.

"This is Kolchak."

"You got the money in that box under your arm? The one you carried when you got off the bus?"

The voice was low, hoarse, male, and obviously disguised. "I do. But how do I know I'm buying two thousand dollars' worth of information?"

"You got the credit card, didn't you?"

"Sure, but…"

"We'll give you more. Take my word for it. But quit crapping around and do like I tell you or the deal's off. Hang up and walk outside. A bus marked Brentwood will be along in about five minutes. Get on that bus and ride to Mitchell Street. Get off at Mitchell and walk four blocks west to a tavern called Jimmy's. We'll get in touch with you again there."

The man hung up.

Except for two old ladies and a sleepy teenager, the Brentwood bus was empty. I dropped coins into the box and sat down behind the driver.

"Let me know," I said, "when we get to Mitchell Street."

"You sure that's where you want to get off?" the driver asked. "On this route, we intersect Mitchell just beyond the industrial district. There's hardly anything there but warehouses and the old air force plant that closed after the war.

Maybe you want the bus marked Harrison. That intersects Mitchell just before you reach the big shopping center…"

"No, this is the right bus."

We joggled along on 18th for perhaps two miles. Then the bus turned left and hummed down an empty road bounded on both sides by industrial facilities. Beyond the industrial district we hit a dark stretch of warehouses and old loft buildings.

The driver braked.

"This is it."

"Thanks."

I climbed down. The door shut. I watched, standing under a single street light, as the taillights faded away. Ahead of me to the west, an immense, deserted complex of buildings loomed on both sides of the street. The old air force plant, no doubt. It covered the equivalent of two city blocks. Far beyond the plant, a tiny neon sign flickered, the only hint of human habitation in this area. That, I presumed, would be Jimmy's.

I started down the narrow street, walking at a normal pace, the shoe box cradled under my right arm. As I neared the middle of the block, shadows encompassed me. At an alley I stumbled, barely righting myself.

The more I thought about my situation, the less I liked it. The people I was dealing with had been almost childish in their approach. The mysterious note in my mailbox. The telephone call to The Cave, telling me to get on a bus and ride to another tavern. If I had chosen to alert the police, Van Doyle would have had no difficulty at all covering me this far. He would have tapped every phone in The Cave; he would have filled The Cave with plain-clothes men; he would have overheard the call and sent squads to quietly cover the intersection at Mitchell before my bus arrived; and he would have infiltrated Jimmy's with more plainclothes men before I got there.

If the man planning the arrangements had been stupid enough to fail to anticipate those contingencies, he could also be stupid enough to think he could take two thousand dollars from me without giving any information in return.

I tightened my grip on the shoe box and balled my left fist.

Even so, I was not entirely prepared when the blow came.

My first warning was a slight scraping sound behind my right shoulder. As I tumbled to my left, a heavy object crashed against the side of my head. The blow blinded me momentarily but I managed to roll over, brimming with contempt for the crudity of the attack, and with rage for the weeks of frustrating effort that now found me wallowing in a gutter.

I opened my eyes. A big man stood over me, his arm raised. Behind him, I caught a glimpse of another man. Both had been hiding in a doorway, waiting for me to reach them As I had rolled I had pulled my revolver from its holster. I pointed it vaguely in the direction of the big man and squeezed the trigger. There was no time to aim properly. I had no idea where the bullet would go. At this range, I figured I ought to hit the man somewhere.

The gun's report echoed and re-echoed along the narrow street. The big man howled and dropped his weapon. He staggered backward. I wouldn't have to worry about him for a while.

The man behind him scurried away. I kneeled, grasping the revolver with both hands. I cocked the gun, I fired, I cocked it again, I fired again.

My target disappeared around a corner. I had an impression of a small, crablike, and very frightened man. Naturally, my last two shots had missed. Even with a target gun I am a poor pistol shot, and aiming at a moving target with my short-barreled revolver, I had probably sent both bullets heading for the moon.

The man I had hit put his right hand over his left shoulder. He sat down on the curb. It was too dark to see his face. Surprisingly, nobody had rushed out to investigate from Jimmy's down the street. Nobody appeared from any other direction, either.

I pointed the gun at my captive. I cocked it again.

"You make one wrong move," I said quietly, "and I'll kill you."

"Sure enough."

The voice, high and in pain, certainly did not belong to the man I had talked to on the telephone. This voice was edged with an unmistakable hill-country drawl.

"What did you hit me with?"

"A sock. Full of sand."

"How long were you waiting here?"

"Half an hour, mebbe. My buddy, he came here a few minutes ago, on the Brentwood bus before yours."

"Get up. Walk ahead of me to the street light. I want a better look at you."

"You bet. I don't fool with a man with a gun. I don't like guns, mister. They scare me. If I knew you had a gun, I'd never had got mixed up in this."

Moaning, the man rose. He moved slowly toward the street light, dragging his feet. I picked up the shoe box with my left hand and followed. He was 6'3", at least, and he wore rags. He weighed an easy 220.

Under the street light, I ordered him to stop.

"Now turn around."

He did so. I gazed into the face of Clay Street. His eyes were sunken, glassy, and lined with black. He needed a shave. His jaw hung half open. A bum, an alcoholic, and probably, a mental defective.

"What," I asked, "do you know about my brother?"

"Your brother?" The big man appeared sincerely perplexed. "Mister, how could I know anything about your brother? I don't even know who you are."

CHAPTER 7

My CAPTIVE TALKED readily. His name was Luke ' McNair. An itinerant railroad worker, he'd been in the city just three weeks. He rolled a drunk in an alley one night and an old man named Sam witnessed the theft. Sam followed Luke into a bar. He bought Luke a beer and told him he knew an easy way to make money.

"He said all I had to do," Luke whined, "was hit a man on the head. I wasn't to kill you. Just hit you, see."

"Where does Sam live?"

"The Garden Hotel."

"He didn't tell you about the note? Or the credit card?"

"No, sir. He said you were an insurance collector. And that once a month, after you paid some calls on Clay Street, you stopped off at Jimmy's on your way home to collect from a night bartender. All Sam told me was to be here tonight. Hey, my arm, it hurts bad…"

"You can stand it awhile longer." I shoved the gun back into the holster. So long as I watched him, Luke would be in no condition to take the gun from me. My only worry now was that a stray squad car would come by and the police would stop and ask questions of two obviously suspicious characters.

"Let's go," I said.

"Where to?"

"I see a phone booth on the next block. I'm going to call a cab. You and me, we're going to the Garden Hotel."

I dialed the Moreland. If I telephoned a cab company dispatcher, I might run into trouble. Many drivers would balk at coming out alone at night to a location as isolated as this. I couldn't waste time waiting for Sam Alban to appear in the Moreland cab line either. So I identified myself to the doorman and asked him to send any cab in the line to pick us up. The driver, I added, would get a big tip for his efforts.

Luke sat down on the curb again. I lit a cigarette. Luke began to moan. I told him to shut up.

"You do as I tell you," I advised, "and after we talk to Sam, I'll let you go. When that cab gets here, you get in first and don't open your mouth. When we reach the Garden Hotel, I'll get out first and you come right after."

"I gotta see a doctor."

"After I let you go, you can see anyone you like. You can tell them whatever you like. If you want to tell them I shot you and why, that's okay too. A prison term for attempted extortion won't do you any harm."

"All we wanted was your money, mister. A couple hundred dollars. I told you about Sam, why don't you let me go now?"

"Is that what Sam said I'd be carrying?"

"He said three or four hundred, and we'd split."

"The box under my arm," I said, "contains two thousand dollars."

Luke received the news in stunned silence.

"I'm afraid," I added, "Sam got you involved in something over your thick head. But that's your tough luck. I'm interested in much more than protecting my money. That's why, if you try to cross me in any way, I'll shoot you. With absolutely no hesitation."

The cab arrived in twenty minutes. The doorman had selected a driver who worked for Sam's company and out of the same garage. The driver knew who I was.

I told him to take us to the alley adjoining the Garden Hotel and to let us out there. The Garden was on the 600 block of North Clay, in the skid-row district. If the driver observed Luke's bloody arm, he didn't comment.

At the Garden I gave the driver a twenty and told him to keep the change.

Like a docile Saint Bernard, big Luke followed me out of the cab.

"Where's Sam's room?"

"Second floor, 205."

"When we go in, head straight for the stairway. You can hold your arm. But try not to let people see the blood."

We walked inside and crossed the lobby. Two old men reading newspapers didn't even glance at us. The desk clerk glanced. But since we seemed to know where we were going, he did not call out.

Luke preceded me up a battered wooden stairway which was illuminated by dirty 25-watt bulbs. A few guests had set their radios or television sets at full blast. Others were noisy drunk. The racket suited me fine. We stopped at 205. The box of money was under my left arm. With my right hand, I pulled the gun from its holster. I jammed the muzzle against Luke's ribs and flattened against the wall.

"Okay, Luke," I whispered. "Now you put on an act."

"Whatever you say, I'll do."

"Knock on the door. Tell Sam you're alone, you want to talk to him. Stand up close so if Sam opens the door with the chain locked, he'll see you but not me. Pray he lets you in. Because if he doesn't, I'll pull the trigger and then shoot my way in. Is that clear?"

"I reckon so."

Luke knocked. He got no response. I prodded his ribs with the gun. He knocked again.

Inside the room, someone shuffled toward the door.

"Yeah?"

"It's me. Luke."

"Luke who?"

"Quit stallin'. You know Luke who. Lemme in, I'm bleedin'."

Sam opened the door a crack. He saw Luke but didn't see me. He closed the door, unlatched the chain, and opened the door wider.

I'd been waiting for that.

I rammed Luke with my left shoulder, shoving him forward. We plunged into the room together. Luke stumbled and sprawled to the floor.

I kicked the door shut and pointed the gun at Sam. Sam huddled in a corner, gazing venomously at me. Sam was very short, maybe sixty years old or more, with thin shoulders and a bent posture. His narrow face was mottled and lined with tiny blue veins. A filthy sports shirt hung outside his unpressed trousers.

I waved the gun's muzzle.

"You're Sam, right?"

"What's the idea?"

Luke sat up. He grabbed his arm again. He groaned.

"Come off it," I snapped. "The big slob told me everything. How do you think I got here?"

"Mister, somebody made a mistake," Sam said. "I never saw that big guy before, except in a bar once. Sure my name's Sam, but I don't know what you're talking about."

Luke said, "Sam, you didn't tell me he had a gun. He ain't no insurance collector. And you didn't tell me about no two thousand dollars, neither."

"The guy is nuts." Sam spat angrily. "He's trying to pin something on me. And who are you, busting in here and waving a gun around?"

I moved a step closer to Sam.

"I see you're packing. You figure on checking out?"

"I was just..."

When Sam got that far with his reply, I rammed him across the cheek with the barrel of my pistol. Sam crumpled, hands over his face. He sobbed.

I leaned over Sam.

"Old man," I said evenly, "you do know something about my brother. Not much, because if you did, your information would really be worth two thousand dollars. But you tried to parlay what little you do know into two thousand dollars by hitting me on the head and robbing me outright. For that I could kill you. I will kill you, unless you tell me how and where you got that fragment of Ed's credit card."

Sam pulled his hands down. He stared at the blood on them.

Luke said, "You better do it, Sam. He means it. He's plumb crazy."

As the old man spoke I listened mute with growing hatred for this animal who could have come forward with what he knew fifteen months ago when the trail was fresh. Instead, he had hoarded his pitiful store of knowledge in the hope of profiting from it one day. Thanks to Sam's greed, his information was useless now, except in theoretically reconstructing a general picture of what had happened to Ed.

"I'm a pensioner," Sam explained, "and I'm always a little short of money. So that night I tied in with this bottle gang. I never did make it back to the hotel. I fell asleep under a stairway in an alley. A couple blocks north of Clay and Jackson, behind the fourteen-hundred block. Early in the morning, a garbage truck woke me up. Private truck or city scavenger, I don't remember. The truck was nearly full and the wind was blowin' so hard, a bunch of trash blew off the truck. This credit card blew almost in my lap. It was burnt away on the bottom. It musta been in a trash fire before someone dumped it in the garbage. Seeing it was a credit card, I stuck it in my pocket. Even if it was burnt, maybe I could calculate a way to use it. I went back to sleep. Then later I read in the papers how this Ed Kolchak disappeared. The name on the card was Ed Kolchak. Well, what could I do? A man like me, if I went to the Clay Street Precinct with the card, they'd hit me with hoses, they wouldn't believe how I got it. So I kept it, see. I almost forgot it and then I heard how you were lookin' for your brother. I don't know what came over me. I never did nothing like this before and I didn't mean no harm…"

"Of course you didn't. All you meant to do was squeeze every last dollar out of that card you could. And I bet you have a police record a mile long. Why did you cut the burnt part of the card away?"

"I didn't want you to guess I just found it in an alley. I wanted you to think I knew more than that about your brother. But honest, I don't…"

"That garbage truck. Was it coming from north to south? Or south to north?"

"I couldn't recall."

"I ought to split your skull open."

"I'm telling the truth."

"Exactly. For what you've done, a split skull is what you deserve. And if I ever find out you're lying, I'll give you that and more. You believe me?"

Sam didn't reply. He didn't have to. He believed me.

Business was slow at The Dugout that night. I could have had my pick of tables, but I selected a booth in the bar instead. I'd changed to a white shirt, tie, and sports jacket. The gun and the box of money were upstairs in my apartment. For once I'd have welcomed the company of a hard-drinking clown like Harry Bagwell. Harry would keep me from thinking the thoughts I was thinking now. But Harry was not in sight.

"A drink, sir?"

Tony posed the question. A Puerto Rican boy, he was tall, smug, slim, and in his early twenties. He'd been assistant cook in the old days, before Bagwell staggered in with his pot of gold. Tony had been paying a lot of attention to me lately. Whenever Lorene or her father were absent or otherwise engaged, Tony, in his faultless tux, acted as greeter. He fawned on me so much that I mailed his name to Max Fuller. All Fuller's report showed was that Tony came from an impoverished but honest family, and that his hobby was constructing little plastic model sports cars.

Of course Tony's concern with me could have stemmed from his interest in Betsy. On the few occasions I'd brought Betsy to The Dugout, his eyes never left her. He'd been at her elbow every second he could. And once he asked me a lot of questions about the girl: where she lived, where she worked, and particularly, whether or not she had any boyfriends.

"I'll try a double martini, mixed the way Bagwell likes them. When that one's gone, bring me another."

I did eat, finally. And as I sobered up on my third cup of black coffee, Lieutenant Van Doyle slipped into the other side of the booth.

He asked, "Been here all night?"

"Most of it. I was out making the rounds earlier. Why?"

"Just wondering." Doyle lit a cigarette.

I studied the dapper detective. Fuller's assessment of him had been concise. "Van Doyle," Fuller had written, "is one of the smartest men on the force. No other man on the force is entirely sure whether Doyle is honest or not. As a result, nobody entirely trusts him but everyone is willing to work with him."

Doyle was forty-five years old. The youngest of seven children, he grew up on Clay Street. His father drove a coal truck; his mother died when he was twelve. He held a number of odd jobs after high school. Then, with a little help from Hiram Schell, he was appointed to the police department. There was nothing significant in Schell's sponsorship of Van Doyle, which amounted to some tutoring for the police exams and assistance in filling out forms. Schell guided hundreds of Clay Street boys through the municipal red tape surrounding appointments to the police and fire departments, especially boys from big families that would provide plenty of voters. Schell's motives may have been politically inspired. But at least he helped those boys into potentially honest employment, something nobody else in the city seemed willing to do.

Patrolman Doyle volunteered for army service in early 1942. He was assigned to the CID and shipped to England, where he spent the war doing work he was still not allowed to discuss. Before his discharge, he made master sergeant. In 1944 he married an English girl who died four months later in a buzz-bomb raid. He had never dated a girl more than twice before he met her; he never dated any girl after she died.

Doyle rejoined the department in 1945. He became a detective in 1946, a sergeant in 1950, and a lieutenant in 1957. He had won nine commendations for meritorious service and had been wounded twice—once, by a dope-crazed teenager, and the second time, by a man who had just murdered a neighbor with a rifle. Doyle had been night-duty lieutenant at the Clay Street Precinct since 1960. His superior, Captain Ernest Ware, was regarded as the most corrupt captain on the force, but somehow Ware's taint never fastened itself onto Doyle. Doyle got along with Ware and the other crooked cops. He was also known as a scrupulously tough guy who commanded respect from the polyglot people in his precinct for his fair enforcement of the law. Apparently Ware liked having Doyle around because when Doyle ran the precinct during the critical night hours, the precinct ran smoothly. Doyle had few close friends. He lived alone in a small apartment at 301 Harper, a block west of Clay and three blocks from the Clay Street Precinct. His only known eccentricity was a fondness for fine clothes.

Tony approached our table. Doyle shook his head. Tony faded away.

"It's been a busy night," Doyle observed. He looked me in the eye. "Among other things, a shooting. A poor dumb hill slob named Luke McNair showed up at the mission with a slug in his arm. He claimed a guy took a pot shot at him while he was walking down an alley. But that doesn't make sense. Nobody on Clay Street would waste a bullet on Luke McNair."

"Sounds like a puzzling case."

"It is. We did some fast checking. Luke's new in town. But he's been seen around with an old crook named Sam Cartwright, who has a record of petty offenses going back to nineteen-sixteen. Sam lives in the Garden Hotel. Know where it is?"

"I've passed it."

"Sure. Anyhow, we went to the Garden and learned Sam checked out tonight. The desk clerk said Sam's face was cut up and bleeding when he checked out. He also said Luke went up to Sam's room earlier tonight with another man. The clerk said Luke was holding his arm, as though maybe he'd been shot. He gave us a rough description of the man with Luke. You know what?"

"What?"

"The description fits you exactly."

I picked up my coffee. I drank deep.

"That's a coincidence. But no kidding. I never heard of this Luke before. Or Sam either. You ought to find Sam. Maybe he could solve the mystery."

"We found him. At a bus station. His story is that Luke and a man he'd never met before went up to his room to persuade him to join a bottle gang, and he turned them down because he was leaving tonight to go to a place with a drier climate, for his sinus. He said he cut his face falling against a coathook in his closet. We provided him with medical attention. But if he doesn't change his story, I guess tomorrow we'll have to let him get on a bus for Tucson."

"Maybe he's telling the truth."

"Possibly. Of course we've been watching Sam, off and on, for a couple months."

"Why?"

"He got drunk one night in the presence of one of my undercover men. He bragged that he knew a way to get a lot of money out of you."

"What did you do about that?"

"We hauled him in. We searched his room. But we didn't find anything and he didn't tell us anything. We assumed at the time he was just talking big. A lot of old men on Clay Street like to talk big. It makes them feel young again."

"That's interesting. I'm sorry I can't help you."

"So am I. I'd hate to think of any private citizen in our town taking shots at other citizens, clobbering more citizens with a gun barrel, and then refusing to tell the police about it. Wouldn't you?"

"Yes."

"I also thought I'd tell you," Doyle added slowly, "that what I ought to do is knock you on your ass here and now and haul you down to the station. Asking questions is one thing, but shooting people is another. This isn't Tombstone in the eighteen-eighties. This is here and now, and nobody in my precinct is going to take the law into his own hands. If I had an ounce of brains I'd get a search warrant, find the gun in your apartment, break Luke and Sam down, and learn the whole story. But before I decide to do that—you got anything you want to tell me?"

"Well, since you asked," I mused, "there is something you ought to know. I obtained this earlier tonight." I pulled an envelope from a jacket pocket. "Here. A portion of one of my brother's credit cards is inside."

Doyle opened the envelope.

"It might be a good idea," I added, "if your crime lab went over it. Not that I expect they'll learn anything. But just to be sure we don't miss a bet."

"Where did you get this?"

"A man gave it to me. A Clay Street drifter. He's been holding it all this time, afraid to give it to the cops, because he thought they'd work him over. But he finally got up enough nerve to give the thing to me."

"How did he get it?"

"It blew off a garbage truck into his lap, early the morning after Ed disappeared. The man was sleeping off a drunk in an alley about 1400 North, behind Clay Street. When he found the card, the bottom half had been burned away. For some reason, he clipped that portion off."

"I see." Doyle frowned. "Presumably, then, someone on Clay Street burned your brother's credit card late the night he disappeared or very early the next morning. And with it, presumably, all his other credit cards and everything else in your brother's wallet."

"I figure it that way too. And you know what else I think?"

"What?"

"I think," I said, "that if there was any doubt before, it can be forgotten now. My brother was murdered. He could have dropped his watch somewhere and some innocent party could have picked it up. But now we know someone deliberately burned Ed's credit cards, deliberately tried to destroy evidence of Ed's existence, hours before the story of my brother's disappearance was made public. Concealment of murder is the only motive I can deduce for that. Moreover, I don't think Ed was murdered for the money he carried. If the killer—or killers—wanted money, I think they would have tried to use the credit cards and traveler's checks somehow, instead of burning them. And I confess, in a perverse way, I'm relieved. Knowing Ed was murdered simplifies my problem. All I have to do now is find his body. And figure out who murdered him—and why."

I did not sleep easily that night. Doyle gave me a pass on the shooting of Luke McNair. Luke, I learned later, had a record of two convictions for mugging, and Doyle probably guessed accurately at the circumstances surrounding the shooting. At 4 a.m. I climbed out of bed, stuck a cigarette in my mouth, and reached for a match.

The match book on the side table was empty. I had several matchbooks in my jacket pocket and I fumbled for one of those. The book I pulled out bore the dignified imprint of the Midtown National Bank and Trust Company. I had no recollection of where I had picked it up. I did not think much of the incident at the time.

BOOK THREE: AUGUST

CHAPTER 8

Irma Bronson rubbed her eyes and stifled a yawn. She perched on a chair beside a second-floor window overlooking Clay Street, her feet resting on a radiator. She wore a blue print blouse, a billowy skirt, bobby socks, and tan-and-white loafers. In silhouette, the baker's daughter's strong features were surprisingly attractive. Hers was a placid beauty, reminiscent of the hefty maidens of antiquity whose profiles adorned ancient coins and trinkets.

Irma said, "I'M sorry. But it's like the other times. I don't recognize anyone down there. I think I'm too far away anyhow. And it's time for me to go home."

"It's only five," I said. I sat on a chair behind a battered desk. The walls and floors were bare. In one hand, I held a warm can of beer.

"I know. But I told my father I'd be home by five thirty. The girl tending the counter for us goes home for supper then."

"You could spare another hour."

"No. I don't want my father to start wondering. He thinks I'm uptown, shopping with friends. If he knew I was here with you, he'd be furious."

"You're a grown woman." I tried to keep impatience from my voice. "You're old enough to lead your own life without getting your father's permission for everything you do."

"I realize that." Irma swung her feet down and smoothed her skirt. "And my father isn't as domineering as you think. It's just that he feels very strongly about this. He's a shy man. He hated it when the newspaper reporters interviewed us, after the police told them we found your brother's watch. I won't try to explain it to you. But I don't want to worry my father now. Ever since my mother died, he's had enough trouble on his mind."

"Sure." I smiled. I finished the beer and tossed the empty can into a cardboard box alongside two other empty beer cans. "Anyway, I appreciate this. I know it's probably a waste of time, but there is a chance you'll spot one of your regular customers down there. If so, the odds are fair that customer is the person who lost my brother's watch in your bakery."

"Would that be so important—finding the person who lost the watch?"

"I think so. I think my brother was murdered near here. I know his credit cards and identification were burned near here. I think the killer, or killers, kept the watch because it looked untraceable, like a million other old Time-0 watches. Nobody bothered to open the watch and see the name scratched inside. But after someone lost the watch in your bakery, you put up a sign saying the owner could claim the watch by identifying the name inside the case. Whoever lost the watch probably saw the sign, but didn't dare come forward. That person guessed quickly enough whose name would be in there. Nobody claimed the watch because the person who lost it either killed my brother or knows who did."

I donned sunglasses and pulled a lightweight hat low over my brow and left the office first. The name on the door was Kay Enterprises. Half the other offices in the building were vacant. Third-rate tenants occupied the remainder. Most of those were already empty and locked, although the one-man export-import firm banged on his typewriter as I passed.

The rickety old two-story structure had no elevator. I walked down a flight of stairs and out onto Clay Street, a half block north of Jackson. Irma and I always left the building separately. The last thing I wanted was to be spotted near the building with Irma, since her picture had appeared in the newspapers when the watch was found. Word would get around, and the person who lost that watch might avoid Clay and Jackson like the plague. Irma had written me a short note three weeks earlier, volunteering to help me without her father's knowledge. She promised to telephone for details later. By the time she called, I'd already rented the office through Max Fuller, and Irma and I worked out our security precautions then.

At Harrison, a block north of Jackson, I turned east and walked three blocks to a parking lot. To get in and out of this lot you dropped a quarter into a slot which activated a gate. In the lot, I'd parked Sam Alban's family car. I borrowed the car from him because his cab, No. 444, was as well-known to Clay Street's denizens as I was.

I drove out of the lot toward Clay on Harrison. But a block before Clay I turned left down a narrow residential street. I pulled up beside a fire hydrant. I sat there, the motor running, waiting for Irma. Her instructions were to leave the building five minutes after I left, walk on Clay to Jackson, walk down Jackson to this street and then walk to the fire hydrant. I calculated that if she followed my schedule, she'd arrive at the hydrant about the time I did. But she'd been ten minutes late the first two times. She was going to be late now, too. Just as she'd been late when I picked her up near the bakery that afternoon.

I sighed. I turned the motor off and lit a cigarette.

Unhurried, Irma rounded the corner twelve minutes later. I opened the door. She climbed into the car.

"I thought you wanted to get back by five thirty," I said. "It's almost that now."

"I had to get ready," she explained. That ended that. It dawned on me that Irma was like a number of other girls I'd known. She was a chronic late arrival.

In silence I battled the rush-hour traffic. At two minutes before six I parked beside a high stone fence surrounding a school two blocks from Bronson's Bakery. Irma peered in both directions.

"I guess it's all right. I don't see anyone who knows me." She opened the door.

"I wish we didn't have to do it this way," I said. "You sneaking around with me near your own home, as though we were committing a crime."

"It can't be helped."

"When do you think you could try it again?"

"Not for a while. I'm not sure. I'll let you know."

"Next time," I suggested, "let's watch during a different time span. We were in the office from one until five the first three times. Next time, I'd like you to watch through the rush hour and into the early evening. Until nearly dark. A different crowd of people turn out then."

"All right. I guess I could tell my father I'm going uptown to have dinner and see a movie."

Irma closed the door. She walked away.

Sam Alban lived five miles across town. I drove to his apartment building and parked in front. I went upstairs and gave the car keys to his wife. A dumpy, amiable woman, she made me comfortable in her kitchen and gave me a cup of coffee and a piece of pie. We exchanged meaningless pleasantries while Sam's two boys, twelve and fourteen, wrestled in the living room in front of the television set.

At seven exactly, Sam's cab pulled up in front of the building. He tooted his horn. I went back down and climbed into the rear seat.

"Thanks, Sam. Let's go to my place. I don't know when I'll need your car again."

"Any luck?"

"Not yet. But were just starting. Did you have another talk with the cab driver who thought he saw my brother's ring?"

"Yeah. But it's like he told you." Sam wheeled into traffic. "He thinks he gave a ride to a fare wearing a ring like that a couple months ago. But he doesn't remember what the guy looked like or where he took him. Just the ring. This cabbie spent two years with the occupation in Japan and he spotted the ring as something special."

"Well, at least it's something. That's two reports on Ed's ring so far. The CGL director Pete Ordway introduced me to didn't remember where he saw the ring, either. But he'd spent military time in Japan, too, and he knows some of the language. He told me he recognized the brotherhood symbol. This director goes to business and social functions all over the state. He thinks he saw the ring on a man's hand at one of those affairs. He meets so many people he couldn't recall the circumstances."

"That ain't much help."

"I disagree. We've found two people who think they've seen the ring now. And with your cabbies, Betsy's girlfriends, and those CGL guys on the alert all over town, if anyone is wearing that ring in public, we're bound to get him sooner or later."

Lorene had invited me to a free dinner at the restaurant that night. The Dugout was expecting an important guest—Jerry Gourmet, restaurant columnist for the Journal. Unlike restaurant columns in the city's other newspapers, Gourmet's column could not be bought by signing an advertising contract. Gourmet visited restaurants whether they advertised or not, and he wrote up only the best. Consequently, Gourmet's column was the only one in town with significant influence on the dining public.

Martin Moss, the restaurant's public relations man, had persuaded Gourmet to give The Dugout a trial. Moreover, while Gourmet's visits were supposedly unannounced, Moss managed to learn the date and hour. To be sure Gourmet was served properly, Lorene was remaining at the restaurant through the evening instead of going home to Jackie at four thirty as usual. She also asked her friends to be there when Gourmet arrived to provide a respectably full house. On ordinary summer week nights, The Dugout was often half empty. Martin Moss didn't think empty tables would help impress Gourmet with the restaurant's apparent success.

Lorene met me at the door. Her eyes were bright, her cheeks a little flushed.

She winked and said, "The great man has already arrived. He and his wife are drinking martinis and they both ordered stroganoff. Pop's going to help me prepare it personally."

"From the looks of the crowd, you don't need me here."

"I know. Most of the investors came with their families. But thank God, Harry Bagwell couldn't make it. Harry invited me to a party Friday night, by the way. He's our moneybags, I guess I'll have to go. Wanna be my escort?"

Lorene asked the question lightly. But it meant a lot. For the first time, she was willing to see me away from the restaurant.

"Sure. I warn you, though. I don't think Harry likes me."

"Harry won't bite. Not at his own party. Anyhow, I'm damned if I'll go up to Harry Bagwell's apartment alone, even if a hundred other people are present."

I shared a house table with Martin Moss and a girl he had hired recently to assist him. The girl's name was Joan Engstrom. Nervous and intense, she was in her early twenties. She wore a suit, but the garment somehow accentuated her very feminine curves in almost blatant fashion. Joan was a Clay Street girl, a petite brunette with a small nose, narrow lips, and a strong chin. Joan had worked as a secretary for half a dozen small advertising and public relations firms, trying in vain to talk herself into a more responsible position, before she saw Moss's classified ad for a "Writer—Female." Joan convinced Moss to give her a shot at the job. While her obvious ambition and drive no doubt impressed Moss, her undeniable physical attributes may have played a role in his decision too. Moss, the devoted father of four, was squeezing Joan's hand and whispering in her ear as I approached. Joan laughed.

I pulled up a chair. Moss glanced at me with momentary annoyance. Then his big round face relaxed into a bland smile. He was a shaggy, bear-like man, and for all his tasteless tactics, apparently a man of basic good humor. He was also uninsultable. I had insulted him the first time I met him and had heard Bagwell insult him a half dozen times. But Moss refused to take any cutting remark to heart. I had long stopped hating him for trying to induce me to plug one of his night-club clients on television during my first week in the city. Charitably, I concluded that Moss simply didn't know any better.

"Hi, Kolchak. You know Joanie. Been hitting the Clay Street dives again?"

"A few. Tell me. How are you going to explain your presence here to Jerry Gourmet? He's just around the bend and he's bound to see you. His visits are supposed to be surprises."

"Hell, I already told him the food is so good I eat here every night." Moss waved for service. Tony appeared. Moss ordered a round of drinks. "This will be a good deal for Lorene and her old man. A write-up from Gourmet will draw people from all over town. And the Journal will include The Dugout in its annual restaurant guide."

"Lorene deserves it. She and her father work pretty hard, trying to build up this place."

"Restaurants are a miserable business," Moss philosophized. "Worse even than mine. You gotta work morning to night, seven days a week. Trust anyone else and they'll steal you blind."

Joan Engstrom had pulled away from Moss. Coolly she surveyed me. I sensed she had me categorized as a potentially dangerous oddball who would never be in a position to help her up the ladder of success. But she condescended to recognize me by remarking, "Lorene likes you, doesn't she?"

"I'd like to think so. But I've been too busy lately to really find out."

"She does, though. I know. Lorene and my older sister went to high school together. Lorene always ignored men. Always waiting for the right guy, I guess. She dated Pete Ordway awhile in high school, but I think that was just because Pete was captain of the football team."

The notion of wiry Pete Ordway playing football struck me as unreasonable. But then, Ordway had probably been a tough, dogged little competitor.

"Pete," Joan went on, "took it hard when Lorene married that air force lieutenant. But when she came back with the baby, Pete asked Lorene to marry him. He was just starting his night law courses then. He worked in his father's drugstore. Lorene turned him down. I guess Pete got over Lorene, though. He's got two kids of his own now. As for Lorene, after the lieutenant she never looked at another man until you came along."

I had to smile. "Good grief," I said. "I've never seen Lorene except in the restaurant."

"She sits down and talks to you, doesn't she?"

"Yes, but…"

"Lorene," Joan said, "hasn't made small talk with a man for years, except to ask how the food tasted or if the service was good. The bachelors in the Clay Street Junior Chamber of Commerce call her 'The Iceberg.' The way she warms up to you is the scandal of their monthly luncheon meetings."

During our meal, Moss discussed his dream. He wanted to publish a Clay Street newspaper, supported with advertisements from the street's more expensive night clubs, strip joints, and restaurants. The publication would capitalize on Clay Street's notoriety and stress entertainment news. It would be distributed to every hotel in town. The only hitch was, few of the night clubs, strip joints, and restaurants Moss approached with his plan displayed even the remotest interest.

But Moss kept plugging. Now he was considering toning down entertainment news and going in for neighborhood social items and strong political editorials. The only neighborhood newspaper then circulating around Clay Street was part of a chain and took no editorial stand on anything. Moss figured that if he took an editorial stand supporting Hiram Schell, Schell might reciprocate by helping line up advertising or even by providing some capital of his own. Schell had not enjoyed the full support of any newspaper of any kind in more than twenty years. The novelty of the situation, Moss hoped, would appeal to him. So far, though, Schell hadn't nibbled.

I recalled, from Max Fuller's report, that Phil Amber owned two night clubs and one restaurant on Moss's list of clients.

"What," I asked, "does Phil Amber think of your scheme?"

Moss looked embarrassed at the mention of the gangster's name.

"Yeah, I know Phil. They say bad things about him, but I never had no trouble. A real gentleman."

"Sure."

"It would help if Phil would get all his joints to take ads in the paper. But as for outright financial backing—I couldn't accept money from a source like that."

Tony walked to our table.

"Sir," he said to Moss, "Jerry Gourmet has finished his meal. He is talking to Mr. Heineman and his daughter now, and it was suggested you join them. Mr. Gourmet liked the stroganoff very much." Tony turned to me. "Jerry Gourmet wants to meet you, too."

"Thanks," Moss said. He dug into his pocket. "Here's something for you. For taking care of us."

There would be no check since we had been sitting at a house table. The restaurant was picking up the tab for our food and drinks. But Moss, as is customary, was tipping Tony for the service.

The tip slipped out of Moss's hand and fell behind a coffee cup. Quickly Tony reached for it. But before Tony's fist closed, I noted that Moss had given him a folded twenty-dollar bill.

Twenty dollars, I reflected, was at the very least four or five times more than the circumstances called for.

Jerry Gourmet's real name was Mike Quinn. An immense, square-faced, deep-voiced, blond man, he was chief of the Journal's copy desk. He had developed an interest in food while traveling around the world during the war in the Military Air Transport Service. "Jerry Gourmet" was a pen name invented years earlier to cloak the identity of the author of the Journal's restaurant column. When Quinn quit the Journal or got tired of dragging his wife out to eat at a restaurant every week, someone else on the Journal staff would become Jerry Gourmet.

Quinn had learned, while questioning Lorene and her father, that I occupied the upstairs apartment and was then seated right around the corner with Martin Moss. Like every good newspaperman in town, Quinn knew all about me. And since as copy chief he never got a chance to cover stories any more, he welcomed the opportunity to attempt to squeeze something newsworthy out of me as a surprise for his city editor in the morning.

In a friendly way, I fended off all his questions.

Quinn grinned.

"Okay," he said. "So you won't talk. I don't blame you. Good luck, guy. I'd like to see you bust the case. There's just one thing I always wondered."

"Such as?"

"What's our chief crime reporter got against you?"

The crime reporter for the Journal was George Nesbitt, the man I'd knocked down in the Moreland Hotel.

"You think Nesbitt has me on his hatchet list?"

"I know it. After you held that press conference, Nesbitt tried to slip some stuff through the desk that would have given you grounds for a libel suit. I killed it, and any other deskman would have too. But Nesbitt wouldn't do that if he didn't have it in for you."

"We had a misunderstanding," I said. "But I don't think it would be my place to discuss it."

"As you wish. I ought to warn you, though, Nesbitt has a long memory. If he dislikes a guy, he might wait years for the right circumstances, but if they arise, he'll crucify you."

"Would your publisher let him get away with that?"

"That's something it's not my place to discuss. All I can tell you is, Nesbitt is no amateur. He's not popular, but he's smart. He's been on the police beat so long he's practically a member of the force. He browbeats policemen into telling him things they wouldn't tell anyone else. When Nesbitt nails you, he nails you good. So if I were you, I wouldn't even risk an overtime parking ticket. If Nesbitt finds out about it, he'll use it as an excuse to dig into your life and drag up every piece of dirt he can find."

In the morning, John Heineman served me coffee. Lorene was spending the day at home with Jackie. Heineman moved away from me without a word. He reached under the bar, pulled out a bottle, and poured himself a drink.

A little before noon I took off for the 500 block of North Clay. That area was pure skid row. I wore appropriately old clothes.

At 2:30 p.m., as I walked out of a bar where I'd interviewed four drunks and a dope addict, a little sports car pulled to the curb. The young man at the wheel waved and said, "Hey, Kolchak!"

I didn't recognize him at first.

"I'm Collins. Don Collins. I met you at the bankers' convention, remember?"

"Oh, sure." We shook hands. "Quite a coincidence, your seeing me here."

"It's no coincidence. Betsy's been trying to reach you. When you didn't answer your phone, she called me and asked me to come down here and look for you. You weren't hard to find. Every loafer on the corner back there knew where you were."

"What's up?"

"Betsy," Collins said, "has found a girl who saw a man wearing your brother's ring. The girl saw the man just two weeks ago. And she can describe him perfectly."

CHAPTER 9

Don Collins drove me to my apartment, where I quickly changed into a suit, white shirt, and tie. I also telephoned the Moreland doorman. I told him to send Sam Alban to an uptown department store where Betsy was modeling in a fashion show and to instruct Sam to circle the store until I came out.

Collins deposited me at the store's main entrance.

"Sure I can't be more help?" he asked.

"You've done plenty already. I really appreciate this."

"Any time. If you want to return the favor, ask Betsy when she's gonna break down and let me take her to dinner."

Collins grinned and drove off.

On the store's third floor, I waited behind an audience of women as Betsy and the other girls paraded in fall styles. At the show's end Betsy slipped out from backstage. She wore a red cocktail gown. Her little face radiated excitement.

For privacy, we elbowed through the mob to a quiet stairwell.

"This girl called me at the agency right after lunch," Betsy said. "And I wanted you to know about it right away."

"The girl who saw the ring called you?"

"No. The girl who called didn't see the ring. But she has one of your sketches, and she found another girl who saw the ring. A girl who works at a key club. The Memphis."

Betsy said her friend had just obtained a job at the key club. A waitress there identified the sketch immediately. A man wearing a ring with that design had been in the club two weeks earlier.

"The waitress is a girl named Nora White," Betsy added "I don't know anything about her, but my friend says Nora comes in at four o'clock for the cocktail crowd."

I glanced at my watch. It was five after four "That's wonderful, Betsy. My cavalry really came through. You're a real princess."

Impulsively I pulled her toward me and kissed her forehead. She looked up, closed her eyes, and half-parted her lips.

Hastily I pushed her away.

"Don Collins," I said quickly, "wants to take you to dinner."

Betsy opened her eyes. She sighed. "Oh, him. I went out with him once and on the way home he got fresh. I don't ever want to go out with that boy again."

"Well, he was pretty nice, taking off from his own work when you called and driving all the way down to Clay Street to find me. I think we owe him something. Why don't you let me buy you both a dinner?"

"If that's what you want."

"It is. And I love you—like a brother."

That was a dirty crack after all Betsy had done for me. And the statement wasn't entirely accurate. I still remembered every detail of Betsy as she'd looked the first time I'd seen her, padding around Ronnie Layne's apartment in a bikini. The memory was anything but fraternal. But I was pushing thirty-six and she was only twenty. And how silly can a practically middle-aged guy get?

Cab No. 444 rounded a corner two minutes after I walked out of the department store. Sam stopped. I climbed into the back seat.

"The Memphis Club."

"Sure." Sam got the cab rolling. "You a member?"

"No."

"I ought to warn you. It's kind of exclusive. It's three miles from here, not far from the convention hall. They get a lot of convention business. But memberships are a hundred bucks a year and the guys at the door don't fool around. You can't just bribe your way in."

"That's a thought. Pull up at the first place with a telephone."

Alban parked in front of a drugstore. I got out, walked into the store, and entered a telephone booth. Max Fuller would be napping at this hour. I dialed his home.

The elderly woman answered.

"This is Mr. Kay. I want to talk to Max right now."

"Just a minute."

I waited perhaps twenty seconds.

Max Fuller said, "Yah?" He sounded sleepy.

"Mr. Kay, Max. I want to get into a place called the Memphis Club with a minimum of fuss and bother. I have to interview someone who works there. Can you help me?"

"Is that all? Christ, when you get there, just tell anyone who asks that you're Mr. Culpepper's guest. By the time you arrive it will be all arranged."

Fuller hung up.

I returned to the cab. In seven minutes, Sam slowed before a spotless, rectangular, two-story concrete building. The first floor was windowless. A white canopy over the sidewalk bore no identification. The only hint of what lay inside were the words "Memphis Club" in silver script on a plaque near the entrance.

A doorman helped me to the curb.

I said, "I'm Mr. Culpepper's guest."

"Oh, yes, sir!" the doorman exclaimed. "We've been expecting you!"

The interior was roomy, contemporary, and thickly carpeted. I crossed a lobby and lounge area to a small bar. At this hour, business was still slow, but it would pick up soon.

The bartender could have been either a professional halfback or a doctor of philosophy. Probably he was a little of both. He sized me up with cordial X-ray eyes.

"Hi," I said. "Where's Nora White?"

"She's working private dinner parties upstairs tonight. Sir, are you a member?"

"No."

The bartender smiled. "I didn't think I remembered you." No doubt he had memorized the names and faces of every one of the club's hundreds of members. "We have strict rules about the girls during working hours, I'm afraid. Might I ask…"

"I'm Mr. Culpepper's guest."

"Why didn't you say so? I'll get her for you."

I settled in a plush booth. The bartender dialed a number on the house phone.

Nora White was long-stemmed and blond, with the proud, confident carriage of a professional beauty. Like the other girls at the Memphis, she was costumed in high heels, black net hose, and a satin, leotard-like garment decorated with lace where it didn't matter and cut very low at the bodice. Gazing at Nora as she approached, I could understand why the Memphis maintained strict rules for its girls. If they didn't, they'd have to summon the police riot squad every night.

"Sit down," I invited.

Nora slipped into the booth. "What's this all about?" Her tone was wary but polite.

I held out my right hand.

"I'm told you saw a man wearing a ring like this one."

"Oh, you're the fella. The one looking for his brother." She studied the ring. "It's been more than two weeks, but I'm positive it was an exact duplicate of the ring you're wearing."

"Tell me about him."

"I'll be glad to. It was a Saturday night. The club was packed. We have a big room on this floor that offers cafe-type entertainment at night—singers, jazz, sick comics, and all. I was working that room. This man was with two other men at a back table. I'd never seen any of them before, they weren't club members. This man was drunk in a nice way, if you know what I mean. He was quiet and happy, always smiling. Well, the room was so crowded, it was hard to move around. This man reached out and pinched me once when I was trying to squeeze past his table." Nora smiled. "He didn't pinch hard, though. Some other men who'd do that, I'd call the manager. But this little guy looked so friendly and harmless, I just looked at him and said, 'Shame on you,' or something like that, and walked away. But a while later he pinched me again. I figured it was time to let him know I wasn't included with the price of the drinks. I reached back and slapped his hand. But I busted a fingernail on the ring."

"He showed you the ring then?"

"Yes. He was terribly apologetic. He held his hand up and said, 'Gee, you must have hit this.' I got a good look at the ring. I was going to have him thrown out, too, but he seemed so sorry about what happened that I forgot it. He didn't bother me any more. When he and his party left, he came over and said, 'Look, I've got a fine wife and four daughters at home, including one almost as old as you. And I'm sure you're as nice a girl as they are. I acted like a fool tonight and if I ever come back here again I'll try to resemble a gentleman.' And when I went to his table, I found twenty-five dollars under his empty glass."

"Describe this man."

"Middle-aged. Short. Five-six, maybe. Thin. A crew cut. Gray hair. A big nose and a big jaw. A deep voice. A real amiable expression on his face all the time."

"Anyone sign for the tab at his table?"

"No. They paid cash. Which is why I'm sure none of them belonged to the Memphis. A member would sign the tab and be billed at the end of the month."

"Could you describe the two men with this fellow?"

"I'm afraid not."

"If they didn't belong to the Memphis, how could they get in?"

"The place was full of nonmembers that night. There was a trade show going on at the convention hall. Many firms in this city maintain memberships here for executives and salesmen. Whenever there's a big trade show, a member like that might come in with a big party of guests, clients, or customers, and the party might split up inside the club. Or a member might even arrange for guests to be admitted in his absence."

"You think this man had something to do with the trade show?"

"I'm pretty sure of it. I do recall that when one of the other men at the table reached for his wallet, a convention badge fell out of his pocket. A plastic-covered name tag with a blue ribbon hanging from it."

The convention hall parking lot was almost deserted when we got there, but I took a chance on finding someone who could help me anyway. I was in luck. The director was still in his office, conferring with his chief of maintenance. When the conference ended I introduced myself and told the director who I was and why I was there.

Apparently the director was an avid newspaper reader with a good memory. He knew all about me. Thoughtfully he tugged at his ear.

"Doggone. I can't help you much. We did have a trade show in here two weeks ago Saturday. Furnishings, appliances, and housewares. And to get in, you did have to wear a plastic badge with a blue ribbon. Thousands of people exhibited or attended the show, though. I sure wouldn't recall any short, crew-cut man with four daughters. But tell you what. Why don't you go see Joe Hale? Joe was in charge of the exhibit space during the show. He knows all the exhibitors, at least. And if Joe doesn't recall the man you're seeking, he might be able to help you find someone who does."

"Thanks. I'd appreciate it if you wouldn't tell too many people about my visit here."

"Don't worry. I'll telephone Joe first thing in the morning, to let him know you're on the way. And good luck."

Irma Bronson called my apartment that night.

"I'm sorry," she said. "The girl helping out in the bakery this summer is going on a vacation with her family. She won't be back until the eighteenth. So unless you want me to come down there on a Sunday…"

"No, a weekday would be much better. Ed disappeared on a weekday. But that's all right. I might be tied up with something else for a while anyhow. Let's make it Thursday, the twentieth. A week and a half from now. I'll pick you up at four o'clock, the usual place. But this time, after you meet me at the car afterward, I'm not driving you straight home. I'm taking you to dinner instead. You ever eat hamburger stroganoff on wild rice?"

"No."

"Well, I guarantee you'll like it."

Joe Hale worked out of a small office in the business district. He was heavy-set, thick-jowled, and cordial. I pulled up a chair across from him at ten in the morning. He lit a cigar and listened as I described the man Nora White had seen wearing the ring.

"No," he drawled, "I don't know the guy. He wasn't an exhibitor. But if he was at the show that Saturday, it's almost certain he's connected with the industry somehow. The general public wasn't admitted until the following week. The odds are good at least a few of the exhibitors might know him."

"Do you have a list of exhibitors?"

"Sure. I already dug one out for you. Here." Hale handed me some mimeographed pages. "Names, addresses, everything. But there are more than a hundred firms on that list, many from suburbs or downstate towns. It would take you weeks to check each exhibitor out thoroughly. I could suggest a possible short cut."

"What's that?"

"Try the trade associations first. And don't limit yourself to associations the exhibitors might belong to. The exhibitors are all manufacturers or distributors. If I were you I'd check associations whose members sell furnishings and housewares to the public as well. That way, instead of concentrating on a hundred or so exhibitors, you'll be covering groups whose members would have been at the show as buyers, too. The executive directors of those associations know all their members pretty well. In a day or two, you could talk to a dozen men who, between them, are personally acquainted with everyone of consequence who might have had business at that show."

Hale prepared another list and in two days I interviewed nearly every trade association official on it. Some, like Hale, were immediately cooperative. Others wanted no part of me, but I obtained their reluctant cooperation by hinting that if they didn't go along, policemen and newspaper reporters would be around soon asking the same questions.

I talked to the last man on the list early the afternoon of the third day. Like the others, he had been unable to identify the wearer of the ring.

"I'm afraid," I sighed, "that wraps it up. I hoped one of you trade association guys could help me. But I guess I'll have to start visiting every exhibitor at that show, one by one.

"Who have you interviewed so far?"

I gave him Hale's list of trade groups. He studied it.

"Yeah. Well, it's a pretty complete list, Mr. Kolchak. But there's one association Hale forgot. Home builders. They buy in big volume, to furnish model homes and equip kitchens and bathrooms. The office of their regional association is right down the street."

The executive director of the home builders' association was out of town. I considered telling my story to his secretary, but decided I might have less trouble if I employed a mild deception instead.

I said: "Look, this is unusual, but maybe you can help me locate someone. A few weeks ago I met a guy in the bar at the Memphis Club. We got to talking. Then I borrowed this guy's pen, to write a check, but I forgot to give it back. I remember the guy said he was a home builder, and that's why I thought I'd try here. He was a short guy with a crew cut, a big nose, and a big jaw. He told me he had four daughters. It's an expensive pen, I imagine he'd like it returned."

The secretary asked, "Was he a real friendly man? Smiling most all the time?"

"Yes."

The secretary laughed. "That," she said, "would have to be Ollie Heywood.

Ollie Heywood was president of Sundown Homes, Inc. The secretary gave me the address and telephone number of his firm. The firm was headquartered in a southern suburb called Crestview.

Sam Alban was waiting outside beside a meter. I signaled for him to remain there awhile longer. In a cigar store booth, I dialed Sundown Homes.

"Mr. Heywood," a girl said, "won't be in today."

"Where can I reach him? It's very important."

"He's at the Crestview Country Club. But he probably won't be back in the clubhouse for another hour or so."

"Is it a public club?"

"No, sir. Members only."

I hung up. I called Max Fuller. I caught him at his office.

"Mr. Kay again, Max. This time I'm going to the Crestview Country Club. Can you get me in, no questions asked, the way you did at the Memphis?"

"Sounds as though you're finally on the trail of something. The Crestview? Let's see. Anybody wonders what you're up to, tell 'em you're Mr. Zalenka's guest."

"Thanks once more." I paused. "I don't want to pry into your secrets, but who in hell are these friends of yours—Culpepper and Zalenka? The biggest spenders on the club rosters?"

"Goodness no." Max Fuller chuckled. "Culpepper owns the city block on which the Memphis Club stands. And Zalenka holds the mortgage on the Crestview Country Club."

The Crestview Country Club was more than thirty miles from the heart of the city, but Sam Alban got me there in less than forty minutes. We traveled a good part of the distance on the Capitol Freeway, a four-lane, divided highway that led to the state capital, a hundred and fifteen miles due south. The afternoon was bright and clear. A mild breeze blew from the west, and the temperature held at a comfortable eighty.

Sam dropped me off at the club's main entrance. He drove to the parking lot. I went inside and told a young man at a desk near the door I was Mr. Zalenka's guest.

"Yes, sir. Mr. Zalenka called a few minutes ago. Can I help you in any way?"

"I want to see Ollie Heywood. You know where he is?"

"I can find out."

The young man spoke to someone on a house phone. He listened a minute and then said to me, "Mr. Heywood's foursome is on the seventeenth green. He ought to be in, in a few minutes."

"When he gets here, would you send him to me, please? I'll be at a table in the dining room, near the door, where you can see me."

What I didn't add was: where I can also see you, and intercept Ollie Heywood in the event he tries to sneak out.

In the dining room, I sat down and ordered a cheese sandwich and a glass of milk. I also told the waitress to send a can of beer and a ham on rye to the driver of Cab No. 444 in the parking lot.

The table had been cleared and I was smoking a cigarette when Ollie Heywood arrived. There was no mistaking the man. Short, slight, crew cut, big nose, jutting jaw. He wore a tan T-shirt, baggy shorts that hung almost to his knees, and knee-length socks. He talked to the boy at the desk for a moment. He turned to stare at me. In a puzzled way he smiled.

He advanced, still smiling. I pushed my chair back and rose.

"I'm Ollie Heywood," he said cordially, in a deep, resonant voice. "But I'm terribly afraid I don't recall who you are."

"My name's Kolchak. Stephen Kolchak."

He didn't even blink. Apparently my name meant nothing to him. He extended his right hand. He was wearing my brother's ring.

We shook. His eyes were on my face. He didn't see my ring.

"We've never met before," I went on. "But we have something in common." I held up my right hand. "We own identical rings."

Heywood raised his hand to make a comparison.

"By golly, you're right. Isn't that the damnedest thing. Where did you get yours?"

"I had it made up special. In Tokyo. Where did you get yours?"

Heywood grinned. He said, "You might not believe this, but the cat dragged it in."

Heywood's apparently flip reply caused me to ball my right fist in anger. I was about to bring it up from the floor when I realized Heywood wasn't kidding.

"My girls have this kitten," he went on good-naturedly. "Well, it's a goddam cat now, but it used to be a kitten. My two youngest used to put the kitten on a leash, like a puppy dog, and romp around the countryside. One day the kitten ran off into a wooded area and got lost. When the kids found the kitten awhile later, it was batting this ring around. It had found the ring in the woods somewhere. The ring was covered with mud, but it had been shiny enough to attract the kitten."

"When did this happen?"

"A year ago last June."

That would have been just two months after Ed disappeared.

"Mr. Heywood, do you think your children could show me that spot? Where they found the kitten playing with the ring?"

"Sure. But I'd like to know why."

"Because," I said, "my brother's body may be buried nearby."

CHAPTER 10

Ollie Heywood, apologetic admirer of satin-clad bottoms at the Memphis Club, proved completely cooperative. I told him my story and while he didn't read newspapers much, he vaguely recalled my brother's disappearance. After the kitten found the ring, Heywood placed ads seeking the owner in his suburban newspaper. When nobody claimed the ring, he gave it to his two youngest daughters. He told them that while he liked the ring—they had presented it to him with considerable fanfare—it was too small for him to wear. Despite his short stature, Heywood's fingers were thick. But at Christmas the two little girls surprised him by paying a jeweler to ream the ring out slightly, so it fit perfectly. Heywood began wearing the ring on occasion, not because he really wanted to, but because his daughters would be heartbroken if he didn't.

Heywood and his wife had been visiting relatives in California when I came to the city and held my televised press conference. Their oldest girl was away at college. The three younger girls, if they saw the stories in the papers at all, failed to relate them to the ring the kitten had found.

Late that afternoon Sam Alban parked Cab 444 in a wooded ravine through which a black-top road wound. At the bottom of the ravine, the road bridged a stream. The ravine was two miles from the Capitol Freeway and less than a mile from the community of large, new, and very expensive homes where Ollie Heywood lived with his family. Yet no sign of human habitation was in view. The trees, casting long shadows, swayed gently. The only sounds were rustling leaves, cawing birds, and chirps from hundreds of crickets.

We climbed from the cab. Heywood's eleven-year-old daughter, oldest of the two who had found the ring, pointed and said, "That's where the kitten was. Near the bridge."

She ran forward. She kicked a spot of turf with her heel. "Right here."

"That's fine, honey." Heywood patted her head. He turned to his eighteen-year-old daughter, the college girl. The other two children were back at the house with their mother. "Catherine, you take little sister home now. I'll be along soon."

The small girl stared at me. "Are you really the man who lost the ring?"

"Something like that."

"Then why don't you know where you lost it?"

"It's a long story," big sister said. "Come on, you."

Big sister dragged little sister away. When they were beyond hearing, Heywood, Alban, and I walked to the bridge and peered down. The water was clear and no more than three feet deep.

"Too shallow," Heywood mused, "to hide a man's body long. If he's here, he was either buried or hidden in the brush."

"The fact the cat found the ring near the bridge," I said, "could mean someone threw the ring over the bridge. He may have thrown other things over the bridge too. The ring's so small, whoever threw it might not have noticed if it missed the water, especially if it happened at night. And I think it happened the night my brother disappeared."

"There's not much traffic on this road," Alban observed. "Where does it lead?"

"It goes on through the woods about three more miles," Heywood explained. "It starts back near the Crestview Road turnoff from the Capitol Freeway and comes out on a state highway. But hardly anyone uses the road any more. The new state highway cuts the time in half."

I asked, "Who maintains this property?"

"The county. Actually, it's part of the county park system. A half mile up, there's a small parking area and a few picnic tables. But even on summer weekends not many people come here. Weekdays it's deserted. Nights, a few kids used to use it as a lover's lane. But that mostly stopped about six years ago when some nut committed a double murder out here. He was caught and electrocuted, but the kids have been afraid to come out here ever since. They go to the drive-in."

Heywood hitched up his khaki trousers. He'd changed to those at his house.

"Well, shall we start poking around?"

"I don't think that'll be necessary." I straightened. "It'll be dark soon anyhow. The police can take it from here, they're equipped for it. I'll drop in at the Clay Street Precinct tonight and tell Lieutenant Doyle about this. He'll set the ball in motion. I'm afraid a lot of people will be coming out here tomorrow. They'll be asking you a lot of questions. They'll talk to your family, too—detectives, reporters, that sort of thing. Think you can stand it?"

"Sure. I'll hide the young ones at their grandmother's. You want the ring now?"

"No. Give it to Doyle. When his men are through with it, you can keep it if you like. Your kids found it and spent their money fixing it up for you."

"Thanks. But after this I'd feel a little nervous wearing it around. If they give it back to me, I'll mail it to you in the city."

We trudged to Cab 444.

"Incidentally," Heywood ventured, "that girl at the Memphis Club…"

"Nora White?"

"Yeah. When she told you she remembered seeing me with your brother's ring, what else did she say?"

"Only that she recalled you because for some reason, you left her a big tip."

"That's good."

I was a celebrity again. Not quite as big a celebrity as the first time. There were no more televised news conferences. But the story of the discovery of Ed's ring and a massive search in the wooded ravine by city and suburban police and volunteer Boy Scouts was played prominently in the next day's afternoon and evening editions. I remained in my apartment most of that day, Friday. Two reporters—from the Beacon and the Express—came up to interview me. But the Journal, the wire services, and the radio and television newsrooms got all they wanted by telephone.

Doyle's first call came at two o'clock. He had been silent, almost angry, the night before when I walked into the station and told him I'd found the ring. I outlined the circumstances and without a word, Doyle dialed the suburban police chief and crisply arranged to organize a search beginning at dawn. He hung up and snapped, "Congratulations. If you'd given your tip to us, we might have found that home builder in half a day instead of the three days it took you. But at least you deserve credit for your damned obstinacy. You can go home now. I'll keep you informed. Unless you want to ride to the suburbs with my men tomorrow and have your picture taken peeking under bushes."

But at two that Friday afternoon, Doyle said, "Kolchak? I'm sorry. But I'm afraid I have bad news."

I drew a deep breath.

"You found the body?"

"No. But we found what's left of your brother's clothes. They were wrapped in a bundle about thirty yards from the bridge. Someone dug a shallow hole in the brush, dumped the bundle in, and then tried to cover it with leaves and dirt. But part of the covering washed away, and some animal started to dig 'em out. The bundle is pretty well deteriorated after all this time, but everything checks—color of the suit, tie, socks, shoes, and topcoat. Even the hat. If we weren't absolutely sure before, we can be now. Your brother was murdered. I was still hoping someone knocked him on the head for his wallet and caused amnesia. But if they stripped him—well, even in summer, he wouldn't get far naked, and that was a cold night in April."

"I appreciate your concern. But I'd already assumed he was dead, remember? I'm through mourning. The clothes going to be much help?"

"Hard to say. They looked like rotting junk. But the crime lab boys can work miracles."

Doyle called again a little before seven.

"We found more, Kolchak. A Boy Scout wading in the stream dug up a cuff link with the letter 'K' embossed on it. We never told you this, but the Chicago police learned your brother bought a set of initialed links two weeks before he disappeared."

"What about the body?"

"I was getting to that. People have been digging up ground out there all morning and afternoon. They'll be at it tomorrow and the next day, too. But I don't think we'll find a body. I think the body is somewhere else."

"Why?"

"We checked the records at the Weather Bureau. March was abnormally cold last year and the first week in April, just before your brother came here, the temperature dropped down to near zero again. The ground was still frozen. That night a guy couldn't dig a grave without professional power digging equipment, not unless he was willing to spend all night on the job. As it was, the guy probably broke his back digging that shallow hole for your brother's clothes. That's why he didn't dig the hole deeper. The ground was like granite. And if he left the body above ground, it would have been found by now. The stream is too shallow to hide a body. So where else out there could it be?"

I had been scheduled to take Lorene to Harry Bagwell's party that night. Lorene called from the restaurant at eight.

"Stephen, if you don't want to keep our date, I'll understand. It's been on the radio all day, what they're finding in that ravine."

"Of course I'm going. I'm dressed and ready."

"If you're sure. I changed clothes in the office. We can leave any time."

Harry Bagwell was in top form. He even looked less haggard than usual. His animated gray face popped up everywhere—over shoulders, under arms, and from behind conversational groups. As a host, he proved a charmer, another of his many inconsistencies—because as a guest at other peoples' parties, he was a holy terror.

Ordinarily Bagwell's working uniform was a blatantly pin-striped suit and an ornate vest. But this evening he'd donned a subdued tux. He was of medium height, and his sparse hair was gray and uncombed. He could have been forty; he could have been sixty. Actually, he was fifty. A network of lines criss-crossed his horsy face. His brows were shaggy and his blue eyes glittered from behind horn-rimmed glasses. A hairline mustache topped his wide mouth.

My first meeting with the attorney had been in June, not long after I moved into the apartment over The Dugout. I took Betsy to lunch at the restaurant and Bagwell occupied a booth behind our table. Lorene introduced us. Bagwell looked at me and drawled, "So you're the new tenant. The man who seeks his brother. Personally, I think you're an idiot. If I lost a relative, I'd celebrate." He turned to Betsy. "I like your friend, though. Does she lay for anyone? Or just for you?"

That meeting ended while Betsy and I sought another table. The attorney had already consumed five martinis and there seemed no point arguing. "If you think he was nasty today," Lorene told me later, "you should see him after he loses a case…"

I'd run into Bagwell in the restaurant a half dozen times since. By then I'd learned his treatment of me had been comparatively cordial. On his periodic binges, sometimes alone and sometimes with courthouse friends, Bagwell delighted in playing the role of a foul-mouthed buffoon. What he liked best was to meet someone with gumption enough to be insulting in return. His rudeness made him a lot of enemies. His temper was quick, and he'd been barred from several of the town's better establishments for brawling. Once he hit a bar girl who resisted his advances. Another time he kicked a doorman sprawling into the gutter.

But Bagwell also claimed a host of supporters. The waitress whose eye he blackened found a new car outside her door in the morning. The doorman's son received a college scholarship. Bagwell gave lavishly to charities. And in the courtroom he stopped playing the buffoon and became an uncommonly brilliant attorney. To the horror of his wealthy and respectable family, he defended the most unpopular clients imaginable: confessed killers, rapists, dope addicts, and anyone else in the kind of trouble that makes headlines. Bagwell loved headlines. He never insulted a reporter. In the courthouse pressroom he was known as "the newspaperman's friend" always good for a drink or a news tip.

He never insulted politicians, either. He cultivated leaders of both parties, but his closest associations were with the mayor's party. It was through those friends that Bagwell reaped sure-thing profits from the purchase of real estate in the path of public works. He also cleaned up buying penny stocks in two bankrupt insurance companies later reorganized by relatives of the state insurance director. And he was one of the few outsiders allowed to invest in a harness-racing association formed by state senators and representatives.

Bagwell's personal life was a mess. He'd been married and divorced twice. Every call girl in the city knew him, and if you were neither a newspaperman nor a politician, he might try to seduce your wife. In recent years his drinking bouts had become more frequent. Perhaps this was because he spent more and more time defending clients sent to him by Phil Amber and other Syndicate leaders, and less on the charity cases upon which he had built his reputation. At any rate, a good portion of his underworld fees had gone to rent and equip his apartment in a penthouse atop the tallest building in a new apartment complex a mile west of Clay Street. And for Bagwell's party, the apartment was packed with well over a hundred guests.

I knew some of them, including a few of Bagwell's co-investors in The Dugout. Martin Moss and Joan Engstrom were there too. Bagwell thought the public relations man vastly amusing. He delighted in vetoing Moss's half-baked schemes for publicity stunts, such as exploding a hand grenade in the restaurant's parking lot on the Fourth of July. Bagwell liked Joan Engstrom because she had the intriguing manner and carriage of an ambitious sexpot. She also caught on fast that there was nothing Bagwell respected more than an insult properly thrown back into his own teeth. "You're pushy, but I'd like to screw you," he told her at their first encounter. "You could," she snapped, "if you'd sober up, take a bath, clean your fingernails, and pay me a million dollars." After that, Bagwell and the girl got along fine.

Inevitably, Lorene and I were separated in the crowd. I bumped into George Nesbitt of the Journal. The reporter's eyes were glazed. He carried a water tumbler with an olive on the bottom and didn't even recognize me. I moved away from him. Max Fuller had noted that Nesbitt got drunk every night, and tonight was no exception. I didn't see any other reporters in the room. During my first week in town, I'd met many of them. Nesbitt must have a special in with Bagwell to make this party. The attorney was taking good care of Nesbitt, too. As I watched, he poured more martini from a pitcher into Nesbitt's glass.

I caught a glimpse of Pete Ordway. He had his hat on and he was walking out the door alone. He must have arrived early. I wondered how he'd come to know Bagwell. Through his political activities, possibly. Around me, much of the talk concerned politics. One of Bagwell's co-investors introduced me to three aldermen, a judge, two state representatives, a half dozen members of a half dozen boards and commissions, and a director of the Clean Government League. The politicians were polite but reserved. They'd seen stories in the evening papers about the discovery of my brother's possessions, and they weren't sure what to say to me. Which made it mutual. I hadn't eaten all day. Bagwell's martinis were taking effect, and I suddenly realized I'd best keep my mouth shut or I'd start slurring my words.

At the first opportunity, I retreated. I put my glass down and began stuffing myself at a neglected table of hors d'oeuvres. I was on my fifth boiled shrimp when I felt a tug at my sleeve.

"Excuse me," a man said. "We've never met, but there's something I'd like to discuss with you. In private. My name," he added, "is Hiram Schell."

Schell and I strolled to a small den. The walls were lined with law books and framed photographs, including a few of our host from World War II days. Bagwell had gone through Officers' Training School and then volunteered for combat, although with his background he could have landed a comfortable desk job. Most of the pictures showed him in fatigues, sprawled on beaches or in jungles holding beer cars. In one, a naked, brown-skinned young woman perched grinning on his lap. Bagwell, I reflected, must have been a helluva trial to his C.O.

Schell closed the door. He smiled.

"You're getting a lot of publicity," he said. He pulled a folded newspaper from his pocket. No doubt he had been carrying it around all night, saving it for this occasion.

"I've seen the stories," I replied.

"I don't mean the stories. I mean the editorial. In the Beacon."

Schell opened the paper to the editorial page and handed it to me. The politician was a tall man in his sixties. Entirely bald, he weighed perhaps two hundred and forty pounds. Despite his age and bulk, he moved with vigor and grace. His wide-lapelled blue suit and broad gray necktie were more than a decade out of style, but on Schell, it didn't seem to matter. The expression on his round face was friendly. With his red cheeks and blue-veined nose, he could have been anybody's rich uncle.

The Beacon editorial was headed law and order? The opening paragraph noted that a private citizen, Stephen Kolchak, had succeeded in turning up through his own efforts an important clue to the disappearance of his brother—a clue the police at the Clay Street Precinct had failed to track down.

One reason for this, the Beacon suggested, was that officers at the Clay Street Precinct were too busy guarding Phil Ambers B-girls to spend time solving ordinary crimes. The editorial ascribed what it termed "the whole rotten police mess on Clay Street" to the influence exerted on the mayor by Hiram Schell, the majority ward committeeman. It said that while Schell had no proven direct ties to the Syndicate, his record of supporting policies and legislation favored by the Syndicate was remarkable. The editorial concluded by reminding voters that in November they could elect an honest mayor who would reform the police department and would not be subservient to Schell.

I put the paper down. I understood now why Doyle had been angry when I first told him about Ed's ring. Doyle had anticipated this.

"I'm sorry," I said. "But I had nothing to do with this editorial."

"Of course not. You were just looking for your brother." The committeeman chewed away the end of a cigar and lit it. "Kolchak, I'm used to these things. Irate editorials. Outraged respectable citizens. The Clean Government League—the Beacons publisher is a CGL director, you know. The publisher and nearly all of his rich CGL friends live in the suburbs. They don't give a damn for the people in my ward. They go home to their split-level palaces and country estates and think how nice it would be if old Schell's ward could be torn down, and we could put apartment buildings there where a better class of people would live—people who could afford to go uptown and spend money in the fancy stores we own, the same stores that take big advertisements in the newspapers we publish. As to where the poor people who used to live there would go—who cares? So they pick on a few B-joints as an excuse to get at me, because I'm in their way. It's part of the game. You understand?"

"Sure."

"Those bastards have been after me for years. A lot of my people are penniless and ignorant. I get 'em on city and county and state payrolls, so they can feed their families. The blue-noses say that's political patronage, that's terrible, how much better it would be for clean government if there were no Schell and those poor people would starve. Then there's Clay Street. Little taverns where a poor man can get just as drunk as the rich man who passes out in the Memphis Club, only cheaper. But because it isn't the Memphis Club, it's sinful. And the strip joints. Personally I'd prefer having department stores on Clay Street, but department stores refuse to move there. They stay uptown and build branches in suburban shopping centers. Strip joints are the only kind of new commercial tenants we can get. And the morons who patronize them and get clipped are getting what they deserve. So what's the crime?"

"My motive isn't to embarrass you," I said. "On the other hand, I have no intention of stopping my search for my brother, either."

"I don't want you to stop. The sooner you learn whatever it is you're trying to learn, the better it will be for all concerned." Schell seemed sincere. "And I'll give you all the help I can. You visit my ward headquarters?"

"I did." It was on Jackson, a half block west of Clay. "The lady there said your headquarters was pretty busy the night Ed disappeared. It was a few days before a primary election."

"That's right. I was there myself until eleven. But I'll send the word out through the organization. It's been a long time, but maybe one of the precinct captains remembers seeing something on the way home."

"Thanks."

Schell flicked ashes to the carpet. "The thing that worries me—it just isn't like the publisher of the Beacon to run an editorial like that so soon after the event. Just a few hours after the story broke. Unless he had some special reason. You don't know of any reason, do you—why the Beacon would be especially interested in you?"

"No," I lied, "I don't."

"I thought not." Schell looked at the floor. "Like I say, editorials don't bother me. But if I thought a private citizen was going out of his way to give me a hard time for no good reason—well, the Fourth Ward can be somewhat inhospitable if I choose to make it so."

I got the drift. It was a warning. And a mighty unsubtle one.

We returned to Bagwell's party.

A man named Updyke approached and pulled Schell aside. I had been introduced to Updyke earlier. Updyke had arrived late and was making up for lost time by getting drunk fast. He was chairman of the state highway commission.

I heard Updyke say, "Hiram, it's all ready to go."

Schell beamed. He steered Updyke away from me. "That's great, Pat. When's the announcement?"

"Next week…"

Lorene found me. We squeezed into a corner.

Lorene asked, "Have you seen Joan Engstrom?"

"Not for a while."

"Martin Moss hasn't seen her either." She smiled. "He's furious. Because Harry's temporarily disappeared, too."

"Maybe he's bathing and getting his million together." I glanced at my watch. "Lorene, all of a sudden I'm starved. I thought I could fill up on those little sandwiches, but I think I need a square meal."

"You idiot," Lorene said softly. "I should have asked if you'd had dinner. Wait'll I powder my nose…"

While Lorene powdered, I gazed idly around the big living room. Updyke, the highway commission chairman, had left Schell. He was talking now to a prominent alderman. The alderman beamed too. He rubbed his hands together. Like a man who has just been told oil is under his back yard.

Behind The Dugout, I pulled Lorene's new blue sedan into a space beside her father's new black sedan. I turned off the lights and set the hand brake. As I reached for the door, Lorene put a hand on my shoulder.

"Stephen—thanks so much. I know a party is the last place you wanted to be tonight."

"I'm all right, Lorene. I was sure long ago we'd never find my brother alive. And it did me good to get out."

"All the same, it was nice of you." She drew me toward her and kissed me. And suddenly she was all woman. Her body strained against mine…

"Oh, God," she sighed. She forced herself away, hands shoving at my chest. "Let's go inside, quick."

CHAPTER 11

Moodily John Heineman poured himself a drink. He had been doing that more and more often before lunch. He perched behind the bar in The Dugout, his big face lined and tired. It occurred to me that John Heineman did not look well. He was overweight, and boozing it up in the morning wasn't going to help his heart condition. But then, booze was an occupational hazard for restaurant managers. Only the smart managers did their boozing in other peoples' restaurants.

I stirred my coffee and asked, "Where's Lorene, Pop?"

"She ain't comin' in today. She's takin' Jackie's Cub Scout pack to a ball game. She'll be here all day tomorrow, though." Heineman was cordial this morning. Other mornings—when he wasn't drinking—he had been treating me with silent, growing hostility. He sighed. "Man, you know something? We're makin' a lot of money now, with our salaries from the corporation. But I never had to work near this hard before. Lorene's young, she can stand it. But I liked it better in the old place. Nothin' to do but pour a few drinks and watch television. But since Bagwell backed us, I been goin' all the time. Watch the employees, buy the food, see to it it's prepared and served right. Then doll up and greet people and stay on your feet until two in the morning. Jeez…"

Lorene's father picked up his shot glass. He downed its contents.

Tony came over. The Puerto Rican boy dumped the morning mail on the bar in front of Heineman.

"Tony," I said, "I want reservations for two this evening. Around nine o'clock."

Tony's eyes gleamed. "Miss Betsy?"

"No, not your favorite photographer's model this time. Someone else."

"Sure enough. You gonna have lunch with Mr. Ordway tomorrow?"

I frowned. "What makes you think that?"

Tony seemed flustered. "Well, you usually do on Fridays. Except for last Friday, when you stayed upstairs. There'll be a big crowd here tomorrow because of a luncheon club. But I can save you a table."

"That won't be necessary."

Tony walked away.

Thoughtfully I stuck a cigarette between my lips. I reached into my pocket for a match. I pulled out one of several matchbooks and lit up, using the last match in the book. I tossed the empty book, which was from the Midtown National Bank, into an ash tray.

Pete Ordway's wife opened the door. Her thin face mirrored surprise. She wore a housecoat and slippers and her stringy, lusterless hair needed combing. She was tall and had a little scar under the left side of her chin, a memento from Phil Amber's teen-aged mercenaries.

"Pete's eating lunch. With the kids."

She closed the door and led me into the living room. "How was the vacation?" I asked. "I stopped at the drugstore last Saturday and Pete's father said you'd gone to a lake near the state capital that morning."

"It wasn't much of a vacation for me. Cooking on a stove that wouldn't work and washing dishes with cold water. But I guess Pete and the kids enjoyed it."

Pete Ordway walked in from the kitchen.

"Oh, hi, Kolchak. I thought we were going to meet tomorrow." He glanced at his wife. "You better get out there, hon. The baby is spilling stuff all over."

"Yeah," Ordway's wife said.

She left. Ordway sat down in an easy chair. I moved some shredded newspapers aside and sat on a sofa.

"I wanted to talk to you about that," I said. "I don't think we should meet for a while."

"What's wrong?"

"That editorial in the Beacon, attacking Schell. It was a dumb play. Schell braced me about it at Harry Bagwell's party."

"You were there too? I had to leave early, to pack for our trip." Ordway chuckled. "Actually, I think Bagwell hates my guts. I got to know him when I was in law school. He set up a small scholarship fund for night students who promised to practice some criminal law, and he screened the applicants himself. I was one of the recipients. We've kept in touch ever since, mainly because I'm on the CGL staff now. He's always pumping me about what the CGL is up to. He wants to relay what he learns to his friends Schell and the mayor, I suppose." Ordway pulled a pipe from his pocket and lit it. "I agree. The Beacon editorial was a mistake. But the publisher did that on his own. He wanted to set things up for later, in case you find your brother and write the articles…"

"I haven't promised to write any articles," I pointed out. "Just to consider writing them. I appreciate your alerting your investigators and directors about my brother's ring. And I appreciate the trouble the CGL took in compiling those lists for me—lists of every Syndicate joint on Clay Street, and of every establishment that's ever been accused of roughing up customers who complained about padded bills. But if you get me involved in your political campaign at this stage, you could do me an awful lot of harm."

"I'll give you another list before you go. Of Clay Street bar, restaurant, and club managers with known criminal records. It took some finagling, but a friend of mine at the crime commission compiled it."

"Thanks. But…"

"I don't think there's anything to worry about. What exactly did Schell say?"

"In effect, that if he learns I'm tied up with your crowd, he'll give me a hard time."

"I see." Ordway puffed on his pipe. "Actually, I bet he already knows you're tied up with our crowd. He's too shrewd to issue an iffy warning like that unless he already knew the 'if' was fact."

"That's a comforting thought."

"Even so, he won't bother you. He's trying to bluff you. He pretends not to mind bad publicity, but the truth is, he hates it. He has an army of grandchildren, and the kids read those stories and editorials. So long as your hands are clean, though, he can't touch you. You've got Schell where you've got Phil Amber. Maybe Schell even consulted with Amber before talking to you. But if Schell tried to harass you, a man whose only activity of record has been to look for a lost brother, the newspapers would murder him."

"Just the same, let's suspend our meetings."

Ordway shrugged. "If you wish." He rose. "I'll get that other list. By the way, what did you think of old Schell?"

"I'd expected an ogre. But actually, I land of liked the guy."

"Most people do. There's a lot of good in Schell and considerable validity to his position. Personally, I'd prefer a wise old admitted rascal like Schell to some of the cold fish at the CGL if it weren't for one thing: Schell lost my vote when he sold out to the underworld Syndicate. And no decent man can compromise with that crowd."

I waited alongside the school twenty minutes before Irma arrived. She wore a flowery blue dress, high heels, and a big hat. Gingerly, she eased into the front seat of Sam Albans car.

"You look very pretty today," I observed. "What's the occasion?"

She blushed. "We're going out to dinner afterward. Remember?"

"I remember. I just forgot you'd have to put on fancy clothes. I hope it wasn't too much trouble…"

"I'm looking forward to it."

I got the car moving. We rode in silence awhile and then Inna said, "Steve, if I don't see anyone I recognize this time, how much longer do you want me to go on?"

"As long as you're willing. But you've already been awfully good about this. If you want to quit…"

"No, I'll help as long as you want me to." She paused. "I hope you don't mind, but I've done some thinking about you."

"I'm flattered."

"Maybe you won't be. Maybe I shouldn't tell you, because it's none of my business."

"Go ahead."

"Well, what happens if you don't learn about your brother? Ever?"

"I don't know. I haven't considered that and don't plan to."

"Maybe you ought to." She regarded me in a pensive way. "There's always that chance. And look at the time you've expended looking for your brother already. Months. A man like you, who's capable of building dams and bridges and roads in places where people need dams and bridges and roads."

"And airfields."

"All right, airfields. You have skills the world needs. You're not using them."

"I didn't realize you were such a heavy thinker."

She looked away and smiled. "I'm sorry. I just think it must be exciting. And rewarding. To go where there's nothing and build something from scratch—something that will stand for a hundred years, maybe."

I didn't reply. Irma, I was discovering, was almost as good a conscience-nagger as Lorene. This unfortunate development I had not anticipated.

"I'll tell you something else," Irma went on. "The last time we were up in the office I asked you what you'd done so far. Among other things you described how those two men tried to rob you. How you shot one and then hit the other man, the old man. Did you have to hit that old man? Are you sure he wouldn't have told you the truth if you didn't hit him?"

"I don't know." Irma was beginning to annoy me. "I was kind of sore at the time. Maybe I should have done it another way, but I'm not going to stew about it now."

"Perhaps you're losing sight of something. Just because your brother is missing, you can't stop being a human being. Maybe you've been spending too much time in those terrible places on Clay Street, with those people…"

"I know someone else," I said, "who told me the same thing. She thinks Clay Street corrupts. That if you're on it long enough, it drags you down to its level. You two girls ought to form a club."

"She sounds like a smart girl. Steve—what was he like?"

"Who?"

"Your brother Ed."

I lit a cigarette with the dash lighter.

"Ed," I said slowly, "was an all-around nice guy. He was a crackerjack salesman because he really liked people. All lands of people. We grew up in a shacktown and some of the kids we played with became bums and criminals and worse. But it never touched Ed. My folks gave him something that made him one of the finest men I knew—kind, thoughtful, and brave, a lot braver than me. He was never afraid to do what he thought was right, as so many of us are. Once he saw a man passed out in a doorway. People kept walking by, pretending the man wasn't there. But Ed crossed the street to look at him. He found a card in the man's pocket. The man wasn't a drunk, he was a diabetic, in a coma. Ed saved that guy's life. He'd help any stranger in trouble and never do the easy thing by turning his back. And he couldn't stand seeing anyone pushed around. When he was growing up he was always coming home with a black eye or a bloody nose, for pitching in with some little guy being clobbered by some big guys. That's the kind of man Ed was—the kind of man I'll never be."

"You must have been awfully close to him. To give up your life this way, just to learn what happened to him here."

"I wasn't close to him at all," I said, "except by mail. I hardly knew him. He was ten when I enlisted in the army in 1944. After that, I went away to college, under the GI Bill. Then to Korea, with the Army Engineers. After Korea I became what some men call a boomer—someone who wanders all over the world looking for new sights and fat pay checks. The pay is high because few men will put up with the hardships that go with the jobs. I'd see Ed for a few weeks between those jobs, nothing more. I guess that's why I have to do this one thing for Ed. If I'd been around, instead of hopping all over the globe, maybe he wouldn't have had so many black eyes and bloody noses. He'd have had a big brother to back him up. When my folks died, he was the only family I had left, you see. So learning what happened to Ed—that's the only thing I can do for him now. All the other things I wanted to do for him—it's too late."

We kept our vigil until a little before eight o'clock. Outside, it was getting dark. Irma could not discern faces any more. The vigil had been silent. I'd brought four cans of beer up to the office, a stifling cubicle on a ninety-degree day like this one. I drank three and Irma drank one. She had spoken her piece in the car. She seemed unusually somber. Me, I didn't have much to say either. I sat and thought about Ed. And how if I ever found the bastards who murdered him, I'd make them pay.

I got up and managed a smile.

"I think we've had it, Irma. Let's go where it's air conditioned and we can relax. And forget my troubles."

"Hamburger stroganoff? I'm dying to try it."

"The place is only a few blocks down. But I'll pick you up in the car as usual. We'll pull into the restaurant lot, so if you're noticed people will think I drove you all the way from the bakery. See you in ten minutes."

"You bet. Steve…" Irma looked at the tips of her shoes. "I hope I didn't upset you. I think I understand now about your brother."

"Don't apologize. And adjust yourself. Your slip is showing."

I walked out into the hall and downstairs. The hall was lighted but the other offices were dark. The building's front door was set so it could be opened from the inside but would be locked from the outside.

I hiked down Harrison to the parking lot and entered the car. I turned the key and pumped the gas pedal. Nothing happened. I tried it again. Still nothing.

I sighed. I climbed out. I poked under the hood a few minutes with a flashlight Alban kept in the glove compartment. I cursed softly when I discovered the trouble lay under my nose all the time. A distributor wire had shaken loose. I shoved it back in place, closed the hood, and got back behind the wheel.

The car started like a bomb. I drove along Harrison to a block before Clay, turned left, and stopped beside the fire hydrant. Irma hadn't arrived yet. I cut the engine and lit a cigarette. When I finished that one I reached in my pocket for another. I glanced at my wrist watch. It was nearly eight thirty. Irma had never been this late before.

I started the car. I drove to Jackson and turned right to Clay. I figured I'd meet her on the way. I turned right at Clay and drove slowly past the building. The office light was out. Irma was not in sight. I double-parked, thinking she'd walk out the door any second. But she didn't.

I circled the block again on the chance I'd missed her. She wasn't at the fire hydrant. She wasn't anywhere.

When I reached the building this time, I parked at a bus stop. I grabbed Alban's flashlight and climbed out of the car fast I unlocked the building's front door and started upstairs, following the flashlight's beam. The second floor hallway was dark. I didn't think the bulb had blown between the time I left the building and the time I returned. Someone had turned the light off.

The door to our office hung ajar.

I pushed the door back. The room stank of whisky. I swung the flash-light beam around.

I saw Irma's big hat first. A falling chair had crushed it. Then I saw Irma. She lay in a corner, nude from the waist down. Her pretty blue dress, what was left of it, had been wrapped about her face and head, mummy-fashion. The dress was damp with blood. Someone had cracked her skull hard.

She breathed with obvious difficulty. But she didn't move.

Two detectives flanked me as we walked outside to a squad car. Irma had already been taken to a hospital in an ambulance. She'd moaned when the attendants lifted her onto the stretcher, but she hadn't regained consciousness.

A big crowd had gathered on Clay Street. A man stepped from the crowd carrying a press camera. I recognized him as Ronnie Layne, in whose apartment I'd met Betsy, centuries ago. He leered and said, "Say cheese, Kolchak." The bulb went off, temporarily blinding me.

He got another shot of me in the back seat, just before the car pulled away.

"What's he doing here?" I asked.

"He picks up his camera," one of the detectives explained disinterestedly, "and runs whenever he hears a siren. If he beats the regular press to the scene, he sells his plates to the newspapers."

We drove to the Clay Street Precinct and parked at a rear door. That struck me as unusual. They wouldn't sneak me in a back door unless they were trying to keep me from the reporters I was sure waited near the front door.

We trudged up a flight of stairs, freshly painted a drab shade of green. On the second floor we entered a small room furnished with half a dozen chairs. I sat down on one of them and lit a cigarette. The two detectives sat down. Another detective joined us.

"How's the girl?" I asked.

"We haven't heard yet," the newcomer said. He leaned against the wall and folded his arms. "Why don't you tell us what happened?"

"I already told these other fellows."

"Sure." He smiled. He seemed the friendliest man in the world. "But you might remember something you forgot the first time. And I'd like to hear, too."

"Where's Doyle?" I countered.

"On another assignment."

"He's the night commander. I think I'd better tell my story to him."

"He's not in charge of this investigation, though." The detective scratched his chin. "Captain Ware phoned. Captain Ware is taking personal charge of the case. I'm Sergeant Grimes." I had heard of Grimes, from Pete Ordway. Ordway had told me Grimes was Ware's bagman—the collector of payoffs from Clay Street dives. "Captain Ware will be around after a while. But you could save a lot of time if you'd tell your story to me."

"Am I being accused of something?"

"Oh, no. We just want the facts. Everything you can recall. Begin at the beginning."

"Well, about four thirty," I said, "we went up there." My hand, I noted, had started to tremble slightly. "You know who I am and who Irma is. She was going to look out the window. To see if she'd recognize anyone from the bakery who might have lost Ed's watch. I stayed with her until about eight…"

"Just a minute," one of the detectives said. "What did you bring up to the office with you?"

"Four cold cans of beer."

"How about the whisky? And the dirty pictures in the wastebasket?"

"I told you. I don't know about that. Someone spilled whisky around and dropped those pictures in the wastebasket after I left…"

"Sure you didn't drink whisky? There's no crime in it. What the hell, if I was up there four hours with a girl, I might have a drink too…"

"May I call a lawyer?"

"If it's necessary," Grimes replied easily. "But I haven't heard your statement yet. If you give me your statement and it checks out, you won't need a lawyer. But you understand, that girl was beaten, raped, and hit on the head so hard nobody's been able to talk to her yet. Under the circumstances, I don't see any reason why you should hesitate to give us a statement. So what did you do during those four hours—when you were alone with Irma Bronson, and she was looking out the window?"

Captain Ware summoned me to his office at one in the morning. Ware, in civilian garb, was squat, broad-shouldered, and round-faced. A Hitler mustache flowered under his button nose.

"Siddown."

Grimes and I took chairs. I carried my coat. My tie was loose and I'd rolled up my sleeves. I was hot, tired, and angry. Teams of detectives had been getting me to repeat my story for hours. Ware himself had entered the interrogation room once and listened in silence. Finally a police stenographer had begun typing my statement.

"Captain," I said, "this charade has gone far enough. For some reason your men seem to think I attacked Irma Bronson. I know my rights. I want the phone call I'm entitled to."

Ware studied me. Then he said, "For *some* reason. Look, guy. We're bending over backward to be nice. Anybody hit you with a hose? Deny you cigarettes? Shine a light in your eyes?"

"No, but…"

"How does it look? You called, we went to this office. We found a dame, raped and slugged. Booze spilled everywhere. Empty beer cans and dirty pictures in the wastebasket. You say you were alone with the girl for four hours. Then you say you left, drove around the block, went back upstairs, and found her on the floor. But nobody saw you enter or leave the building. Hell, man, why shouldn't you be a suspect? And even if you did go out, you could have attacked her before that. Maybe you were drinking, and showed her the pictures. She got sore and you lost control or something. And later you sobered up, drove around the block, and went back to telephone the precinct. It sounds possible to me…"

The captain reached for a big envelope on his desk. He extracted a photograph.

"Recognize this?"

I certainly did. It was a picture of Betsy, one of the many she'd given me. I'd last seen it among the pile of other pictures in my closet. In the picture, a cheesecake shot taken by Ronnie Layne, Betsy wore a bikini.

"Where'd you get that?"

"Your apartment." Ware put the picture down. "A few men and I looked around there earlier tonight."

"You had no right…"

"I had a warrant, that gave me a right. We found all sorts of things. A gun. Lists of business establishments, on stationery with the letterhead of the Clean Government League. Other lists, on stationery from Peter Ordway, a CGL attorney who is active in the minority party. Stacks of personnel investigation reports from a private detective named Max Fuller, including reports on one of my lieutenants, some newspapermen, and many other prominent people, the most recent being Hiram Schell. You are a complicated man, Mr. Kolchak, much more so than you let the world believe." Ware gazed at Betsy's photograph. He licked his lips. "And we found some of these. Dirty pictures, like we found in the wastebasket. Do you collect dirty pictures, Mr. Kolchak?"

"You're crazy! The stuff in the wastebasket, what the detectives let me see of it, was pure pornography. But there's nothing obscene about the picture on your desk. I've seen girls wearing less on a public beach."

"I dunno." Piously Ware shook his head. "I wouldn't bring a thing like this into my home…"

I wasn't sure whether to laugh or cry. I decided instead to strangle Ware.

I would have tried it, too, if the telephone hadn't rung.

Ware reached for it. He listened and scowled. "Okay," he snapped. He hung up and glowered at Grimes. "I thought I told you not to let him call anyone."

"He didn't."

"Then how come Harry Bagwell's outside? Demanding to see his client?"

CHAPTER 12

Bagwell wore his pin-striped suit and vest. He carried a briefcase. He moved and spoke with a matter-of-fact crispness I had never observed in him before. He barked demands at Ware and in two minutes we were alone in a small conference room.

Bagwell waited until the door closed. Then he asked, "First of all, did you do this thing? I don't give a damn if you did. But if I'm going to help you..."

"I didn't do it." I rubbed my forehead. "But before we go any further, I ought to explain. I appreciate your coming here. But I'm not sure I want you as my lawyer."

"You're not?" Bagwell leaned back. "Who else did you have in mind? Pete Ordway?"

I looked surprised. Bagwell snorted in derision. "Christ, Ordway won't help you. The CGL is dropping you like a hot potato. I imagine Ordway has been ordered to dig a hole and climb in until this thing blows over. The only reason I'm here is Lorene tracked me down by telephone and pleaded with me to take your case. Lucky for you, I wasn't out on a bender."

"How did you know about my relationship with the CGL? And Ordway?"

"I guess they haven't told you yet. It's public property." Bagwell opened his briefcase. He pulled out a copy of the Journal. "The Beacon and every radio and television station in town have the story of the rape, and how you're being held for questioning. But Nesbitt of the Journal has a scoop. Nesbitt has the rape—and a good deal more. He and Captain Ware are old buddies, you know. Years ago, when Ware was a sergeant, they patronized cat houses together. As freeloaders, of course. And tonight, Ware told Nesbitt what he found in your apartment."

I unfolded the paper. The banner proclaimed:

KOLCHAK HELD IN CLAY STREET RAPE.

The read-out added:

Police learn "searcher" was spy for CGL.

The two photographs snapped by Ronnie Layne appeared under the banner. A casual reader, glancing at my surly face and the stony-eyed detectives, would have figured me guilty for sure.

Nesbitt's story didn't say outright I was guilty. But it emphasized every fact indicating I could be.

Kolchak admitted drinking beer while alone in the office with the Bronson girl, a buxom, attractive blonde [Nesbitt wrote] but he claimed ignorance of the whisky bottle. Ware said Kolchak also professed never to have seen the pornographic pictures found in the wastebasket. The police captain added that numerous photographs of scantily clad women were among the items found hidden in a closet in Kolchak's apartment. Kolchak, like his missing brother, is a bachelor...

Nesbitt described Ware's search of my apartment as full of surprises, including confidential CGL documents which led police to surmise Kolchak was serving as an undercover prober for the so-called "reform" group while pretending to look for his brother. Also found were documents from Peter J. Ordway, a CGL attorney heavily involved in Fourth Ward politics. A woman who answered Ordway's telephone said Ordway was unavailable for comment. And the CGL's executive director, reached at a vacation hideaway in Canada, said he had no comment at this time but would issue a statement in the morning. Police also discovered more than 60 character investigation reports prepared for Kolchak by Max Fuller, a lone-wolf private detective whose license has been suspended nine times. While police would not disclose the names of the people whose most intimate secrets were probed by Fuller in Kolchak's behalf, it was learned they included prominent politicians, attorneys, law officers, businessmen and journalists. Captain Ware said it is "hard to see where Kolchak could possibly use this material, much of which is libelous and worse, in his alleged search for his brother...!"

Nor was Nesbitt's main story the end of it. A secondary yarn, headed PHOTOG RECALLS HOW "SEARCHER" MADE THREATS, OGLED MODEL, ran at the bottom of the page. Ronnie Layne got his licks back at me and then some. He told an anonymous reporter—Nesbitt, no doubt—how I'd visited his studio shortly after my arrival in the city "to discuss a business proposition."

"According to Layne," the story went on, "Kolchak, who had been drinking during the meeting, could hardly take his eyes from a bikini-clad model in the apartment at the time. Later, Layne said, Kolchak became dissatisfied with the progress of the business discussion, flew into a rage, and threatened to strike the photographer..."

I put the paper down.

"It seems," I mused, "all my chickens are coming home to roost. It's open season on me for every bastard with a grudge, isn't it. Okay, Harry. I apologize for acting like a snob. If you'll still have me, you're my lawyer. I'm learning things. I guess if Ordway wanted to be my lawyer, he'd have been down here hours ago."

"You're getting what's called the treatment," Bagwell replied easily. "Obviously, Nesbitt doesn't like you for some reason, and Nesbitt's publisher is feuding with the CGL. The publisher is a friend of the mayor's, and thinks the CGL meddles in politics too much. But don't let it rattle you. Nesbitt's publisher is a sick, dying old man, and Nesbitt is a professional character assassin who would have been fired from any other newspaper in the United States years ago. You'll survive."

"I thought Nesbitt was a friend of yours."

Bagwell grinned. "All reporters are my friends. Nesbitt is a particular friend. He killed a story once that would have got me disbarred. I've been paying off ever since, with exclusive news tips and with booze. But let's hear your troubles."

Briefly I recounted the events leading up to the moment I found Irma unconscious on the floor.

Bagwell nodded. "I see. You willing to take a lie test?"

"Any time."

"Fine. When the girl comes to she'll probably clear you anyhow. But let's not depend on that. Ware's an idiot. However, the state's attorney and Ware's superiors uptown are not idiots. They'll drop what little case Ware has against you if you pass a lie test. You saw nobody else going in or out of that office building?"

"Nobody. How's Irma? Grimes wouldn't say."

"According to the boys in the pressroom, still under sedation. But she's in no danger of dying. Apparently, she wasn't hit that hard. You know, I can't understand Ware coming down here personally tonight. After you called the precinct, who was in charge of the crew that went up to your office?"

"His name was Leary. But after twenty minutes, a man named Conover came in and told Leary to go back to the station. Conover said it was Captain Ware's orders."

Bagwell frowned. He lit a cigarette. "This gets screwier by the minute. Leary is a good man. But Conover—if Conover weren't Hiram Schell's nephew, he'd be on permanent school-crossing duty where there's no traffic. His regular job is driving Grimes around while Grimes collects payoffs from whores and bartenders for Captain Ware. Grimes collects so much loot he needs a bodyguard, in case some crooks try to hold him up. Twenty minutes, you say. Van Doyle must have been running the precinct when your call came in. Who'd you talk to?"

"Some desk sergeant."

"That would be Olcott. Another of Ware's hand-picked stooges. You identify yourself to Olcott?"

"I gave him my name, yes."

"Uh-huh. Five gets you ten, after he dispatched Leary's squad and called for an ambulance, he telephoned Captain Ware. Your name is well known in the Clay Street Precinct. Olcott is smart enough to know Captain Ware would want to be informed about any case involving you from the beginning. And then for some reason Ware took personal charge and sent Conover out to relieve Leary. Where's Doyle?"

"Grimes said he was on some other assignment."

"That dumb bastard Ware. He's so anxious to build a frame around you he's not even trying to find other suspects. He's buried Doyle somewhere and he's letting Conover flounder around with a sincere but hopeless investigation. What's Ware got against you?"

"I have a theory. At your party, Hiram Schell pulled me aside for a talk. An editorial in the Beacon disturbed him. The Beacon publisher is a CGL director. And Ware is Schell's appointee."

"So that's it." Bagwell seemed genuinely startled. "I should have known. Schell is getting uncommonly sensitive in his golden years. I imagine he left standing orders with Ware to give you a hard time if and when the opportunity arose. The rape was Ware's opportunity—and he's gone overboard trying to please his master. But basically Schell's a fair man. It will be a pleasure to rout him out of bed. Hell listen to me. I think I can convince him to order Ware to let Doyle get going on the case, and send Conover back to his crossword puzzles. Schell won't underwrite an out-and-out frame. Anyhow, the halo's already been knocked off your head. That's all Schell wants, I'm sure. Even if Doyle finds the wino who raped that girl before the night is out, things will never be the same for you in this town."

"I don't think," I said slowly, "Irma was attacked by a wino."

"You don't? That's what I think, taking you at your word it wasn't you. That's what everyone else is going to think—that the girl was attacked by a vagrant who snuck in there and hid until everyone left, so he could break into offices and commit some minor burglaries. It happens on Clay Street often enough. This vagrant saw the girl alone and took advantage of his opportunity."

"Harry, I think Irma was attacked because she was helping me look for Ed."

Bagwell stubbed his cigarette out. "That's an interesting notion. But Doyle will regard it as pretty farfetched. Unless you can prove it."

"What's to prove? It was an obvious frame from the beginning. Sam's car wouldn't start. Someone pulled the distributor wire loose to delay me. Someone left whisky and dirty pictures in the office. It's all too nice and neat."

"Plenty of Clay Street bums carry whisky and dirty pictures. After you left the girl alone up there, that's probably what inspired the guy to attack her. A deserted Clay Street office building at night isn't the safest place in the world, you know. And a wire came loose from the car. You said yourself that if you'd been sharp enough to spot the loose wire right away, the delay would have been less than a minute. If someone wanted to delay you, they'd have let the air out of a tire. Who else knew you were using the office with that girl?"

"Max Fuller. He arranged the rental for me. Sam Alban. Those are the only people I told, and I assume Irma didn't tell anyone. But tonight was our fourth stake-out. Irma or I or both of us could have been seen going in or out of the building earlier. Or we could have been followed. I stopped looking for tails months ago when Doyle pulled his detectives off me. Irma—anyone could follow her and she wouldn't know the difference. Anyone watching either of us would have known I left the building first, got the car, and waited for Irma at the fire plug. My security precautions were lousy. I should have varied them each time, instead of falling into a routine…"

"Don't start blaming yourself. It's all your imagination anyhow. Doyle will probably have a confession from the bum who raped that girl before you eat breakfast. He's a good copper—and so are most of the other guys at this precinct, Captain Ware, Grimes, and that clown Conover notwithstanding. I've already spoken to several of the detectives who watched Grimes interrogate you. They told me they're ready to go out on their own time, if necessary, to look for evidence supporting your story. If you're innocent, they won't allow you to be railroaded. Ware's just making the most of his opportunity while he can. I'll get working on Schell and I'll set things up for a lie test, but unless the girl comes to and clears you, I'm afraid you may have to spend the remainder of the night here. I could seek a writ…"

"A few more hours here won't kill me, if you think we can clear this up early in the morning."

"We can. Sign your statement, but don't answer any more questions." Bagwell rose. "By the way. I'm professionally curious. Who were the prominent attorneys Nesbitt's story said you had Max Fuller investigate?"

"There was only one of real prominence. You."

"That," Bagwell said, "was what I thought."

I read the morning papers while eating breakfast in a cell. In its final edition, the Journal kept Nesbitt's story in the lead position but killed the irresponsible side-bar yarn quoting Ronnie Layne about my visit to his studio. Nesbitt must have slipped that one through the desk when nobody was looking.

The rape was on page one of the Beacon, too, but not in the lead position. The lead story, filed from the state capital, concerned an announcement from the state highway commission of the route for a new limited access expressway. The expressway would completely encircle the city and would connect with all freeways leading out of the city, including the Capitol Freeway. The Beacon had reproduced a four-column map showing where the connections would be made. The connection with the Capitol Freeway, I noted, would be about nine miles beyond the turnoff leading to the ravine where Ed's possessions had been found. Acquisition of land for the new expressway was to start immediately and construction of the road would begin in three years.

The Beacon's account of the attack on Irma was considerably more restrained than the one in the Journal. Bill Totten's by-line was on the story. He emphasized that detectives said my attitude was cooperative. He observed that the official investigation seemed marked by confusion. Detective Sergeant Leary had commanded the team responding to my call, Leary was replaced at 9:05 p.m. by Detective Sergeant Conover, who ordinarily handled administrative affairs, and Conover was replaced at 1:40 a.m. by Lieutenant Doyle, who ordinarily ran the precinct at night but had been ordered at 9:18 p.m. to check beatnik joints for liquor law violations. Totten buried a brief résumé of what Ware found in my apartment in the last three paragraphs.

After breakfast I took a lie test. Bagwell and an assistant state's attorney had completed arrangements for it while I slept. The operator was a civilian, a college-trained interrogation specialist who worked for a private polygraph service. I answered ten yes or no questions which the operator and I decided on in advance. The key questions demanded direct answers to whether I had attacked Irma or had any knowledge of who did.

Bagwell and Van Doyle were waiting outside in the hall when I left the testing room. Doyle's trousers were rumpled for once. The detective's eyes were half-shut. He must have been on his feet all night.

The operator announced, "As far as I'm concerned, this man had nothing to do with the rape of that girl."

"Okay, and thanks," Doyle said. He turned to me. "That test might not be needed any more. But I'm glad you volunteered to take it. It will stop a lot of nasty rumors."

"You found the man who did it?"

"No," Bagwell said, "but they found a witness who saw you walk out of the building, and saw Irma Bronson combing her hair upstairs in that office at the same time. An old man who lives in a hotel across the street. On hot nights he has nothing better to do than sit around in his undershirt and look out the window. He recognized you because he's seen you on Clay Street dozens of times. He was watching you and the girl all afternoon, in fact. He said after you left, he got up to go to the can and when he returned the light in the office was out. He figured the girl had left. He claims he went to bed and dozed off and when he heard the sirens later he thought it was just another Clay Street brawl."

"Actually," Doyle added, "that reporter Totten of the Beacon found him first. This morning we canvassed the occupants of every room overlooking the office building. But Totten thought to do that last night, after he phoned in his story. This old guy denied seeing anything. But he seemed nervous. Totten observed that the old man's chair was beside the window, and an ash tray on the sill was full of butts. So Totten tipped me off before he went home to question this old guy with extra care. After half an hour, I got the old man to admit what he'd seen. A helluva note, when a guy who could clear an innocent man doesn't want to take the trouble because he doesn't like policemen. But that's Clay Street..."

"There'll be a few formalities," Bagwell said, "but you'll be free inside of an hour. Feel up to a visit to the pressroom?"

"Definitely not."

"I'd advise otherwise. Your image could stand rebuilding. But it's your decision. I'll go announce the results of the lie test, so it can make the next newscast..."

Bagwell hurried off. Doyle led me to an office. He opened a closet and hauled out a large cardboard box full of documents.

"Your junk," he explained. He sat down and lit a cigarette. "I'm sorry about that. And I hope you're not judging all the men in this precinct by what you've seen of Captain Ware. He had no business taking this stuff from your apartment. I can't figure what made him go up there in the first place."

"Maybe," I mused, "he knew what he was going to find."

"Seeing more spooks in the corner? Bagwell told me that you think the girl was attacked because of her association with you."

"How is Irma?"

"I got a call from the hospital while you were on the lie box. The doctors allowed a couple of our men to talk to her briefly. She recalls she had her back to the door when the light went out. Someone must have opened the door from the hall, reached in, and flicked the switch—it's right beside the door. Then the man hit her on the head. She started to come to later, when her clothes were wrapped around her face, and he hit her a couple more times. She never saw the man. He didn't say a word. She couldn't even swear it wasn't you. The doctors say she won't suffer any lasting physical damage. It's the emotional damage they're worried about."

Doyle paused. He tugged at his ear. "You know, Kolchak, you haven't done badly so far. You led us to that ravine. But I think this time you're kidding yourself. You hope the attack on Irma Bronson means you're closing in on the people responsible for what happened to your brother. But that's illogical. If those people were really worried about you, I don't think they'd hesitate to murder you, instead of terrorizing Irma Bronson. We don't have any leads to who raped her yet, but sooner or later one of our informants will give us a tip. And it'll turn out to be some sex-starved drifter."

"We'll see. I notice you said the 'people' responsible for Ed's murder. You think as I do, then? That more than one person is involved?"

"I do. That fragment of your brother's credit card blew off a garbage truck in an alley behind Clay Street. The watch turned up in a bakery seven miles away. The ring, jewelry, and clothes were in a ravine in the country, an isolated spot not many people except residents of that suburban area knew about. My own theory is, your brother's pockets were emptied somewhere down on Clay Street. That would have taken just a few moments. Then your brother's body, fully clothed, was loaded into the trunk of a car..."

I glanced sharply at Doyle. "Just a minute. A car had to be involved, to reach the ravine. But why are you assuming the body was transported fully clothed?"

"Oh, yeah." Doyle smiled humorlessly. "We got our crime lab report yesterday. I was going to call you, but then this thing came up. Well, the crime lab found blood on the clothes—your brothers type. They also found a big motor-oil stain on the back of your brother's suit coat. The suit coat was inside the bundle buried at the ravine, with the topcoat on the outside. There was no oil on the topcoat. I think your brother, still wearing his suit, was jammed into the trunk of a car in which somebody had spilled motor oil. His topcoat was probably tossed over him. Then I think he was driven to some other location and stripped. Whoever gave you that credit card told you he found it early the morning after your brother disappeared, didn't he?"

"Yes."

"Okay. I think the killers were anxious to get your brother's body safely away from Clay Street as soon as possible. If it was one man, I don't think he'd have stopped to burn credit cards. I think one person or group of persons did the burning down on Clay Street while another person or group of persons drove off with the body."

"That motor oil could have been from a garage floor. Who carries his own motor oil?"

"I doubt that the killers would dump the body on an oil spot unless it couldn't be avoided. Oil in the trunk of a car—they might not even have seen that until the damage was done. And lots of people buy their own motor oil. I understand it's even available in the finest suburbs, from discount stores and other big-volume retail outlets. You can buy it cheaper that way."

"Then it also figures," I said, "that Ed was stripped before his clothes were taken to the ravine. Probably at the spot where the body was hidden or disposed of. I can't see the killers stripping him at the ravine. They'd have to leave a dead body in a car parked alongside a public road while they buried the stuff. Moreover, if the killers were in a hurry, they wouldn't go any further out of their way than they had to. The place where the body is hidden can probably be reached by driving along the Capitol Freeway. It might not be far from that ravine, in one direction or another."

Doyle nodded. "We thought of that. A driver can make real good time on the freeway. It's only a few hours to the state capital, since the speed limit is seventy. We're checking every sheriff and police chief along the freeway from here to the capital, to see if any unidentified bodies turned up in their jurisdictions shortly after your brother disappeared—bums found crushed by railroad trains, that sort of thing. But so far, nothing. We're not finished with your brother's clothes, though. I wouldn't discuss it with anyone yet, but we've shipped your brother's suit coat to Indiana. A big oil company research lab there often gives us a hand. It's just possible that with their facilities they can tell us more about the oil stain on that coat." Doyle looked down at the carton of documents on the floor. "You know something?"

"What?"

"The report on me in there. To you from Max Fuller. It contains a few inaccuracies, but on the whole Max did a creditable job."

I rode home in a squad car. A patrolman hauled my documents upstairs. When he left I shoved the box into a corner, picked up the telephone, and called the Beacon. Bill Totten was off duty. I obtained his home number and dialed that.

"This is Kolchak," I said. "I just want to say thanks. For going out of your way to help Doyle find the old man in the hotel."

"All in a day's work."

"I bet. I've been reading your newspaper."

"I tried to tone the story down as much as I could. Some of the detectives told me they thought Ware was jumping to a lot of wrong conclusions. But we had to print…"

"Stop apologizing. You should have hit me harder, it would have been a better yarn. I just had a thought of my own. You know your papers banner story?"

"About the route for the new expressway?"

"Yeah. Well, I can't tell you why I think this, and I may be all wet, but if I was a newspaper reporter in this town, I'd persuade my city editor to allow me to look into who's been buying property along the route of that new road. I have a sneaking suspicion certain politicians and their families have been speculating with that land for some time."

That took care of Totten. I'd returned the favor, as best I could.

I called Sam Alban. I told him his car had been hauled to the police garage, and that I'd pick it up, pay the bill, and drive it to his home.

I opened the telephone book. I began looking for the number of the hospital where Irma had been taken.

Someone knocked on my front door.

I opened it. John Heineman gazed down at me. His face was very red.

"I heard," he said, "you came back."

"How's Lorene? I want to thank her for calling Bagwell."

"Never mind Lorene. She's in the kitchen. She don't know you're here yet. I want you to clear out, now."

Heineman swayed, his voice trembled.

"What's wrong, Pop?"

"Plenty. The Dugout is a public place. We can't stand trouble. All the papers said you lived above our restaurant. And you know what happened last night? Our customers saw the policemen going in and out of your apartment. Two squad cars parked right in front. A couple detectives came into the restaurant, too. They asked questions in front of everybody. Martin Moss says that's very bad for us. People will be afraid to eat here. And this morning, first thing, the garbage truck failed to make its pickup. The garbage is rotting out in the alley. Then a building inspector, a fire inspector, and a health inspector came around. All three, within an hour. That never happened before. They all found violations. And they wouldn't take payoffs. That never happened before either…"

I was beginning to understand what Hiram Schell had meant when he told me, at Bagwell's party, that the Fourth Ward could become inhospitable.

"Relax, John. I'll get out tonight." I lit a cigarette with a match from another book from the Midtown National. "I'll go to a hotel."

"You damn well better."

"I'll tell Lorene…"

"Don't tell Lorene nothing. It's better you have nothing to do with her. It was Lorene's idea, your moving up here. I was always afraid of a mess like this…"

Heineman was about to say something else. But he never did. His face contorted with sudden, paralyzing pain. He fell backward, just like that. If I hadn't reached out, he would have tumbled down the stairs.

BOOK FOUR: SEPTEMBER

CHAPTER 13

Betsy leaned back and closed her eyes. I stepped harder on the accelerator and Don Collins' little sports car swung into a gentle curve on the Capitol Freeway at seventy-five per. The morning was cloudless. We were thirty-four miles south of the heart of the city and three miles beyond the turnoff leading to the ravine.

The curve flattened out into a straightaway. No other cars were in sight. I nudged the sports car up to eighty, to eighty-five. I held it there for several minutes. Then I raised my right foot. By the time we reached a turnoff marked river road we were coasting at forty.

At the bottom of the turnoff, I braked before a stop sign.

Betsy yawned. She opened her eyes. She'd fastened her dark hair down with a red scarf tied under her chin. She wore a tight, short-sleeved white sweater and a red skirt.

"That was fun," she said. "Where are we going?"

I snaked the gearshift into first. We turned left.

"A place called Maryville. According to the map, it's eight miles east of here."

"You weren't kidding, were you?"

"I warned you. This is no joy ride. I'm looking for my brother's body."

"Steve, that's crazy. You can't dig up the whole countryside."

"I don't have to. My brother wasn't buried out in the open. The ground was too hard at the time."

"But someone could have dropped him in a lake. Or buried him in a cellar. If he was taken out here at all."

"I know that." We poked along at thirty miles an hour. "But I still think it's worth trying. I think wherever Ed is, he's not too far from that ravine, at some spot reached from the freeway. And I think whoever hauled him out here wanted to do more than just hide the body. I think they wanted to destroy the body, as much as they could. The easiest way to accomplish that would be by fire. So for a starter, I'm canvassing rural fire departments."

"That's a terrible thought. Why would those killers go through all that trouble?"

"I don't know. But then, why were the killers so anxious to get the body away from Clay Street in the first place? Why didn't they just dump it in an alley or down a sewer? What difference would it make if Ed's body were found? Why did the killers think it necessary for Ed's body to disappear?

If we knew that, we'd probably know who killed Ed. And since the killers went to so much trouble to keep Ed's body from being found, I think they took the further trouble of trying to destroy the body somehow."

Betsy yawned again. "All right. Go talk to your country firemen. Poke around old ruins and whatnot. But at noon we're going to eat lunch, aren't we?"

"Sure."

"Fine, I'll talk to you then. My gosh. Why are you driving so slow?"

"Just waiting to see," I explained, "if another car comes barreling down off the freeway to follow us."

No other car did.

Maryville's fire chief sat on a chair in front of the fire station reading a copy of the Beacon. Inside his staff of three polished the pumper. If a fire broke out, one of his staff members would ring a bell for volunteers.

Betsy remained in the car. I got out and approached the chief.

"Hi. I'm Stephen Kolchak. I was wondering if I could see your fire log for about a year and a half ago."

"You could, if you'd tell me why."

"My brother disappeared in the city about then. His clothes were found not far from here. I think it's possible somebody tried to burn his body."

"Oh, you're that fella." The chief rose. "The sheriff said you might be out this way. C'mon." He chuckled. "At first I thought you were another city man tryin' to buy my eighty acres. The new expressway goes right along River Road here, y'know. My land's got water, electricity, and everything. And it's right near where they'll put a turnoff. Perfect place for a motel."

We went inside and climbed a flight of stairs.

"Interestin' stories in the Beacon," the chief continued. "How all those politicians bought up land along the route in advance."

"Bill Totten's stories, you mean? He's a good reporter."

"I reckon. But I knew somethin' was going on long before he wrote those stories. City men started comin' out here and making offers on my land as long as three years ago. They must of had a good idea of the route as far back as then."

The chief flopped behind his desk. He opened a drawer and pulled out a massive ledger.

"There it is. But it won't do you much good." He flipped pages. "After I talked to the sheriff, I took a look myself. The whole month after your brother disappeared, we had only one fire where a body could have been hid in what was left. Jensen's barn. And Jensen hired some boys to come out a few days later and haul the junk away. If there were human bones in the mess, they'd of found 'em."

"What sort of a man is Jensen?"

"A big dumb farmer. He lives with his wife and eight kids. Not to mention his father and his mother-in-law. They got four dogs and a goat. Any stranger would have a hard time sneakin' a body into Jensen's barn, day or night. And Jensen's barn burned down at three on a Sunday afternoon. One of his kids started it, sneakin' a cigarette."

"Well, thanks. By the way. You know anybody out this way uses Mexoil?"

"What's that?"

"An off-brand motor oil." I pulled a Mexoil label from my pocket. "The can looks like this. A bold Aztec design. The stuff isn't marketed any more, but a couple years ago a shipment went to some retail outlets in the city. It was sold real cheap.

"Can't say I ever recall seeing an oil can like that," the chief said. "Not that I think I'd recall anyhow."

Betsy and I picnicked at a roadside table.

"Those four young firemen at Hilltown," I observed, "will never be the same. I don't think they ever saw a real live photographer's model before. They'll probably rush out to buy Brownie cameras and start learning a new trade…" A gust of wind hoisted Betsy's skirt. She howled and dropped her hands to her thighs to keep it from blowing up in her face. In so doing, she knocked her bottle of pop to the ground. This just wasn't Betsy's day.

She glared at the fallen bottle.

"I think you're awful," she said. "All morning and half the afternoon I sat in the car under a hot sun while you talked to fire chiefs."

"Coming along was your idea, not mine. I tried to persuade you to stay home."

"You won't even allow yourself to be seen with me in the city. This is the only way I can see you at all."

"I took you and Don to dinner, didn't I?"

"Sure. Then you skipped out and Don had to take me home. But I don't want to go out with Don Collins. I want to go out with you."

"That can't be done."

"Why not?"

"In the first place, much as I appreciate all the help you've given me, and much as I like you, I don't want you to get too attached to me. I'm too old for you. You should be going out with younger men. Young fellows with prospects. And preferably, with a lot of money in the bank already. Money never hurt a marriage."

"I'm not in the least impressed by that reason. What else?"

"In the second place, I'm afraid to be seen with you. You know what happened to Irma Bronson. I don't want anything like that happening to you."

"I'm not afraid." Betsy looked down. "You ever find out—how she is?"

"Not yet. Her father wouldn't even tell me where she went. But I had Max Fuller trace her. Irma's living with an aunt and uncle in Fond du Lac, Wisconsin. I sent her a registered letter a few days ago. I hope she replies. Her father really has it in for me. When I showed up at the hospital, he tried to take a poke at me. I should have stuck it out and gone up to her room anyway. Instead of leaving because I didn't want to cause any more trouble."

"Everyone else thinks a tramp attacked her. And that you're just imagining she was attacked because she was with you. Even Don says that. And I think so too."

"I don't." Desperately I sought to change the subject. Betsy's affection was becoming too direct for comfort. "Anyhow, you're a wicked woman. Captain Ware of the Clay Street Precinct is my authority for that. He showed me one of your pictures, taken by Ronnie Layne. Ware said the picture was obscene."

"Which one?" Betsy flashed a naughty grin. "The one where I'm looking back over my shoulder? I told Ronnie I thought he was going too far…"

"No," I said. "The one where you're holding up a beach ball.

"The other was much worse. In the other, I didn't have a top on. And Ronnie made me adjust the bottom real low…"

"That's funny."

"What's funny?"

"Now that you mention it, I remember that picture. And it wasn't among the pictures returned to me by the police department."

"You think Captain Ware kept it?"

"I doubt it. Everything else was returned. I checked it very carefully. I just scanned the pictures, but that one wasn't there. If Ware had seen it, I'm sure he'd have displayed it as his horrible example, instead of the one he did pick. Probably Ware never saw that picture at all. Which means it could have been stolen from my closet before Ware and his raiders arrived."

"Who would do a thing like that?"

"I'm not sure," I said. "But I can think of at least one admirer of yours who might qualify"

I parked Don Collins' car in front of his apartment building. It was also my apartment building now. Don had arranged for me to sublease a three-room layout on the ninth floor from a couple on an extended European vacation. Don's apartment was on the twelfth floor. The building was a mile and a half from Clay Street and in a ward controlled by the minority party, so Hiram Schell had been unable to attempt any retaliatory measures against my new landlord. Moreover, this landlord was big enough to fight back. An insurance company worth several hundred million dollars owned the building. Schell would never joust with a windmill of those proportions.

The desk clerk said Don had returned from work. I decided to return his car keys personally.

Collins had peeled his jacket off. He held a drink in one hand. He opened the door and said, "Hi, Kolchak. Any luck?"

I stepped inside. Don's apartment was much larger than mine. He could afford it. His income, according to Max Fuller, was already more than twenty thousand a year. Oddly enough, the people he worked with felt he more than earned his way. Collins had been learning the ins and outs of the office equipment business almost since infancy from his father. He was an honor graduate, with a master's degree, of an eminent school of commerce. Like my brother Ed, he seemed to thrive on the gregarious and highly competitive existence demanded of men who engage in top-level sales. And everybody knew that one day, since he was an only child, Don would become president of M. J. Collins, Inc. Don's private life was about what you'd expect. Most of his close friends were young, competent, well-to-do, and still unmarried. He was no saint—the crowd he ran with numbered several prematurely heavy drinkers, and if Don wanted to spend a night with a girl, he knew which telephone numbers to call—but he held his vices within gentle-manly bounds. His greatest weakness was a fond-ness for plunging in cheap stocks.

"Not much," I said "But thanks for the loan of the car." I tossed the keys onto a coffee table. "It's all gassed up."

"Drink?"

"Why not?"

Collins drew me a Scotch and soda.

"I'll need the car Monday through Wednesday next week," he said. "But Thursday and Friday it's yours, if you want it."

"That's mighty generous of you." I sat down and lit a cigarette. "In fact you've been uncommonly good to me lately. Considering I'm using your car to picnic with your girl."

"I have an ulterior motive," Don replied easily. "Betsy has an awful crush on you now. But I figure the more she sees of an ugly old gorilla like you, the more she'll ultimately appreciate me. Not just for my charm and good looks. But for my father's money. And as for getting you an apart-ment in this building—I have a deal with the desk, see. The minute you try to sneak Betsy up there, the desk will tip me off, I'll bust in and save her honor. She'll thank me for that later, after we're settled in the ten-room bungalow my father will give us as a wedding present."

"Your father might not approve of a girl who grew up on the wrong side of the tracks, whose mother was a waitress, and who works as a photographer's model."

"My father couldn't care less. My mother was working in a laundry when he met her. He walked into the place to sell an adding machine. My old man ran into a friend of yours today, by the way. Pete Ordway."

"Your father's in the CGL?"

"No." Don smiled. "But with an Irish name and a father of his own who was a precinct captain, he just can't help dabbling in politics some. Right now he's with a volunteer group working for the opposition candidate for mayor. Ordway's involved in the campaign too. Didn't your private detective's report on me note that my father is addicted to smoke-filled rooms?"

"No, it didn't." I glanced at a storage recess in an end table. "Max didn't tell me you collected ladies' handkerchiefs, either." I leaned over and pulled the little hanky into view. Neatly folded, it was embroidered with a large butterfly. I asked, "Is this a sexual fetish? Or mere old-fashioned sentiment?"

Collins looked suddenly embarrassed. "Oh, yeah. Betsy dropped it in the car the night you took us to dinner." He got up and walked to the window, his back to me. "I was going to return it. The next time I saw her."

Lorene telephoned at seven o'clock.

"Stephen?"

She sounded tired. Which was understandable. Since her father's heart attack, she'd been running the restaurant all day and night almost every day. Her father had been confined to a sanitarium. Lorene hired a full-time maid to stay home with Jackie.

"You have dinner yet?" she asked. "If not, why don't you drop over here?"

"I'd like to, Lorene. But your father was right. All I can bring you at this point is trouble. I don't think it would be wise even to be seen in The Dugout."

"Schell won't bother us. Harry will get him to leave us alone, like he did before."

"Schell left you alone because I moved out, not because of Harry Bagwell."

"I told you, you didn't have to move. Harry has enough influence..."

"Schell knows Harry has an interest in your place," I said. "He stopped the garbage pickup and sent the inspectors around anyhow. That was Schell's message to me: 'Get out of my ward or I'll hurt anyone who helps you stay.' Furthermore, I'm sure Bagwell would evict me before tangling with his pal Schell. Harry goes all-out for clients, but I'm no longer his client. If I was his tenant and I jeopardized his investment in the restaurant, he'd oust me immediately. And if you don't think Bagwell is a hard-headed businessman, you should see the bill I got for his services."

Lorene sighed. "All right. Be stubborn. And I bet I know another reason you won't be seen here. You're thinking of Irma Bronson. But I don't think I'd be courting danger if you were one of about twenty guests at a party I'm giving, do you?"

"I guess not."

"The party's at noon Saturday. At my house. It's Jackie's birthday. The other guests will be considerably younger than you, but I imagine you'll all get along. And if you buy Jackie a present, don't you dare spend more than a dollar. Can you make it?"

"I wouldn't miss it."

"Fine. I'm taking the whole day off—the first one since Pop went to the hospital. We've hired a new assistant manager, and he can run The Dugout."

"Tony still works for you, doesn't he?"

"Yes, but he's too inexperienced to take full charge. Why do you ask?"

"No reason. See you Saturday."

Nothing in Lorene's voice had betrayed her feelings. But she had just asked me to her home to meet Jackie.

I had a date with Bagwell that night. His penthouse was only a few blocks from Don Collins' building. I had telephoned Bagwell's office to protest the size of his bill. He refused to discuss it on the phone and said he'd be tied up in court the remainder of the week. But he suggested, somewhat acidly, that if I had any complaints, he'd hear them in the evening at his home.

The attorney wore dark trousers and an ornate dressing gown. His hair was mussed more than usual. He smirked and held the door back and asked, "You bring the check?"

I walked inside. "I brought the checkbook. But as I told you, five hundred dollars seems like an awful lot."

"I knew you'd be cheap about it. But then, you always did have the cautious look of a Bohemian with a locked wallet."

Bagwell, the efficient, reassuring attorney I'd met at the Clay Street Precinct, had been replaced again by Bagwell, the sadistic buffoon.

He led me to a sofa. A coffee table held a decanter, an ice bucket, and two glasses. One glass, half-full, sported a big lipstick smear on its rim. On the floor beside the coffee table I observed two high-heeled shoes, two nylon stockings, a crumpled cocktail dress, a slip, a brassiere, and a pair of panties. Bagwell must have made the girl strip for him right there. Fuller's report had been correct: the attorney's sex life verged on the moronic.

"I've been entertaining," Bagwell explained vaguely. He sat down and poured himself a drink. "As for my fee—you forget, I performed some very specialized services. I woke Hiram Schell from a sound sleep and got him to order Doyle onto the case. No other lawyer in town would have dared do that. And a few hours later Doyle found your witness."

I sat on a chair. "It's not that I don't appreciate what you did, Harry. And I certainly expected to pay you for your time. But five hundred…"

"I'll tell you something." Bagwell seemed to be enjoying himself immensely. Behind his horn-rimmed glasses, his blue eyes flashed. "At first I wasn't going to charge you at all. I'd help you as a favor to Lorene, and for the personal pleasure of demolishing a police frame-up." He leaned back. "Then I thought: Here's this Kolchak fellow, throwing God knows how much money down the drain in a crazy search for a long-lost relative. He ought to at least pay me a few dollars. A token bill—fifty bucks, maybe." The attorney picked up his glass and downed a gulp of bourbon. "And that's what I would have charged you—if I hadn't learned how you abused my hospitality."

"What do you mean?"

"The expressway land scandal, that's what I mean. Your pal Bill Totten told half a dozen guys in the Beacon's city room how he got the original tip from you. And city room gossip always gets back to me. It's easy enough to deduce what happened. Old Updyke of the highway commission was at my party and so were you. Updyke got stoned and fell all over himself telling his cronies how the commission was going to announce the route the following week. Updyke's a big-mouthed ass. But I didn't think any of my guests who heard too much would betray him. The only reporter there was Nesbitt, and Nesbitt was too drunk to hear anything but the clink of the martini pitcher. That crazy young idealist Ordway left before Updyke arrived."

I said, "I won't deny it, Harry. I phoned a tip to Bill Totten. I didn't tell him about you or your party. Hell, it was just a wild guess. But in view of the ease with which Totten dug up enough material to expose the scandal, it was just a matter of time before someone else exposed it. Every real-estate agent dealing in properties along the route must have suspected long ago that the smart money from the city was moving in on another sure thing…"

"You're quite right. It was a sloppy deal. So many people got advance word of the route that exposure and scandal were inevitable." Bagwell chuckled. "And such a mixed company! A syndicate headed by Hiram Schell's business partner disclosed as the owners of the old deserted Fly-ways Airport up on River Road, a quarter mile from what will be an arterial turnoff. What a site for a subdivision! Or an industrial park! Right next to the airport, a hundred-acre farm held in the name of the wife of a CGL director. Thieves from both parties jumped in on this one. A logical development, since the highway commission is split four-to-three. The image of that simon-pure minority candidate for mayor might even be tarnished before the scandal ends. And all along River Road, Phil Amber's been buying sites for a future string of hotbed motels."

"I'm sorry if I embarrassed you."

"Oh, I'm not embarrassed. The few people who learn what happened will be sore at Updyke, not at me. But the point is—by phoning your tip to Totten, you proved a rude guest. And I think you ought to pay for that."

I studied Bagwell for a moment. I reached for my checkbook and a pen and started writing.

"Harry, I haven't seen your name in Totten's stories yet. Where did you make your little investment?"

Bagwell's eyebrows arched in mock innocence. "Heaven forbid! I wouldn't get mixed up in anything as shady as that. And even if I did, I'd do what all the really smart boys have learned to do. I'd confine my speculations to a few modest purchases made through a bank trust. Nothing so obviously greedy as the old Flyways Airport, with its acres and acres of flat, juicy, already-cleared land. And behind a bank trust because it would take an act of God before my identity could be disclosed."

I handed him the check. It was for two hundred dollars. Bagwell smacked his lips. I hadn't let him down. He'd have been terribly disappointed if I paid him the full five hundred "There," I said. "It's excessive, but you're worth it. The sum also includes a measure of balm for my lack of social grace. But this is all you'll get."

"I'll accept your check—as partial payment. Got a slip of paper?"

I gave him one. While I lit a cigarette, Bagwell wrote out a receipt. On the receipt he acknowledged payment of $200 toward a debt of $500.

"You pay me the remainder by the end of next month," he said happily, "or I'll turn the balance over to a collection agency. And I'll call Nesbitt at the Journal. I doubt he could print the story, but it would make a helluva headline. Searcher Exposed as Deadbeat."

I rose.

"Where are you going?" Bagwell asked.

"Clay Street. I'm not allowed in Phil Amber's joints any more. Other bartenders seem to have orders to throw me out, too. But I make appearances down there as often as I can. So anyone who wants to can find me."

"Have a drink first."

"I'd rather not. Your guest is probably getting bored, hiding out in your bedroom."

"Oh, she won't mind. I want her to say hello to you…He raised his voice. "Come on out, dear. It's not the vice squad, it's just a friend. Come out, or I'll be very angry, and you know what that could mean…"

A bedroom door opened. Slowly, Joan Engstrom walked toward us. She'd thrown one of Bagwell's robes around herself. She was barefoot. She looked sore as hell.

"I just got Joanie a new job," Bagwell explained. "Beginning Monday, she's going to work at the Harriman Advertising Agency, the biggest in town. Old Harriman is a special friend of mine. Joanie will start as a copywriter, but her future will be bounded only by her ability, or should I say agility, which I have already learned is considerable. You remember Mr. Kolchak, Joanie…"

"Hi," Joan Engstrom said woodenly.

I got out of there fast. Bagwell was exacting his revenge and then some for that crack about his needing a bath. I didn't think many working girls would envy Joan her newfound success.

CHAPTER 14

Tony lived in a rundown apartment building within walking distance of The Dugout. The Puerto Rican boy had left his family and moved there when The Dugout expanded. As one of the original staff, he had been elevated to a position of some authority. And while his new salary wasn't high, it had been high enough to allow him to escape from the communal tenement where he had spent his boyhood.

I rapped on Tony's door at ten in the morning. Under my arm, I carried an attaché case. Yawning, Tony opened the door a moment later.

"Hello, Tony."

I slipped inside. Tony gazed at me with genuine bewilderment. He wore slippers, old trousers, and an undershirt. "Mr. Kolchak. It's nice to see you. But what…"

"I'm glad you're glad to see me. Then you won't mind if I look around."

"Hey…"

I'd already scanned the living room. It was a mess. Clothes and newspapers lay everywhere. Apparently, when Tony lived with his family, his mother had done all his picking up for him. On a mantel he'd arranged about a dozen little plastic model automobiles. From the parts strewn on a card table it was obvious he was assembling another one. It struck me that, like Betsy, Tony was hardly more than a child.

I strode into his bedroom. The bed was unmade. Pin-up pictures filled one wall. I spotted the photograph I was looking for right away. In it, Betsy peered back over her shoulder. She wore no top and her bikini bottom had been pulled low.

"I didn't think you'd hide it in a closet the way I did," I said. I reached for the picture. "Where did you get this?"

"I bought it."

"No, you didn't buy it. You stole it. From my place, when I lived above The Dugout."

"You have no right…"

"Let's talk." I carried the picture and the attaché case into the living room. I sat on a straight-backed chair. "Tony," I said, "a few months ago I'd have been so angry at the notion of you prowling my room that I'd have tried to beat the truth out of you. But I'm learning things. From some real pros. There are other ways to hurt a man."

"Mr. Kolchak, that's my picture."

"I'm not going to waste time arguing. You've had a special interest in me all along. You even figured out that I ate lunch with Pete Ordway every Friday. So here's the deal: If you don't level with me, I'll tell Lorene how this picture disappeared from my closet and turned up in your apartment. She'll take my word for it. She'll fire you immediately. What's more, you'll have a tough time getting a job that pays as well anywhere else. Give The Dugout as a reference and your new employer will be told you were fired for stealing. You won't be able to afford this place any more. You'll have to move back with your family and sleep with all your brothers and sisters on the living-room floor. You won't even be able to afford another model automobile…"

Tony clenched his fists. He sat down and punched his thighs a few times. He looked very worried.

"I'm no thief," he insisted.

"I don't care what you are. A lot of kids make mistakes. I'm not your judge. All I want are straight answers."

"Doggone," Tony said. He got up and shoved his hands into his pockets. He turned away from me. "I never did feel right about it. But I'm no thief. I took the picture because I liked the girl, if you get me. You had plenty of other pictures of her and I didn't see how you could miss that one. But there were times I could have stole money you left lying around, or your gun. But I didn't."

"You went up there often?"

"Every week or so. When I knew you were way down at the end of Clay Street. It's easy to get up there. There's a key to your apartment on the ring in the office."

"Whose idea was this?"

"Martin Moss. At first he paid me five bucks a week, just to tell him everything I heard about what you were doing and who you were seeing. When I told him you were meeting Mr. Ordway, he offered me fifty bucks to sneak into your apartment and look around. I found the stuff from the Clean Government League and the reports from the private detective. Moss gave me a bonus for that. He paid me more money to go back and copy some of that stuff, and to see what new documents you were getting."

"Moss ever tell you why he wanted this information?"

"No. Only that some very important people wanted to keep an eye on you. For business reasons. I got scared after a while, but Moss wouldn't let me quit…"

"Okay, Tony." I rose. "I'll keep my part of the bargain. What you do with your life is your affair, but if you'll take my advice, you'll never get mixed up in a mess like this again."

"Can I keep the picture?"

"No." I dropped it into my attaché case. "It's mine. You can ask Betsy for another one in the same pose if you like. But if you do and I hear about it, I'll break your neck."

Martin Moss nodded to me and went on talking into his telephone. His big face was haggard and drawn. Papers littered his desk. A cigar smoldered forgotten in an overflowing ash tray.

I pulled up a chair. Moss's office was in the front room of a first-floor apartment in a three-story walk-up building. A sign in the window said MOSS AND ASSOCIATES: ADVERTISING, PUBLIC RELATIONS, COMMUNICATIONS. The rear of the apartment was occupied by an old lady who made and sold ceramic coffee tables and ash trays.

"Didn't you get the release?" Moss demanded. Apparently, he was trying to plant a handout for one of his clients in one of the city's newspapers. "I sent it to your financial editor a week ago. I know you get a lot of releases down there, but this one was about Clay Street Home Improvement Corporation. How they're gonna give trading stamps to anyone ordering a new siding job, a kitchen or remodeling job, or a jalousie room addition. That's a good story, ain't it? Whaddya mean, it don't sound like financial news? Who else gives trading stamps? Do the big lumber companies give 'em? The suburban contractors? Hell, no. But Clay Street Home Improvement does. It's a first. Okay, so don't write a big story, just a paragraph or two. Would that kill you? We take ads in your newspaper, you know. We have good friends in your business office. I…"

The man at the other end of the line hung up. Angrily Moss looked at the receiver. He dumped it back on the hook. He shrugged.

"The bastard. But that's public relations for you."

"That," I said, "is a travesty on public relations. You're a living, breathing insult to every guy who ever made an honest buck in public relations. You're no more qualified to call yourself a public relations man or an advertising man than you are to become an astronaut."

"What brought that on?"

Moss sincerely wanted to know. My insult didn't bother him in the least. With a skin that thick, he was bound to succeed at one enterprise or another, sooner or later. Even now, I found myself unable to entirely dislike Moss.

"Marty boy," I said, "I have just had a long talk with Tony. He told me you paid him to spy on me. Don't bother denying it. I'll make you the same offer I made him. Either you tell me a straight story or I'll ruin you professionally."

Moss picked up his cigar. He avoided my eyes. "Whaddya mean, ruin?"

"Just that. I'll call my friend Bill Totten at the Beacon. I'll tell him what Tony told me. Then I'll call Doyle at the Clay Street Precinct. I'll tell him what Tony told me. I don't know what kind of a law you violated, but you must have violated some law, bribing Tony to prowl my apartment. And I still have some news value, my charges will get into the newspapers. Then everyone will know how you took advantage of your role as a public relations and advertising man to spy on one of your client's tenants. You'll have a hard time keeping old clients and finding new ones. Your releases will also be blacklisted at city desks. It'll be a dirty trick on Tony. He doesn't think I'm going to tell anyone else what he told me. But if you want to drag him down with you, that's okay. And when the pressure's on, I think Tony will repeat his story to Lieutenant Doyle."

"Maybe he won't."

"Oh, yes, he will." I held up my attaché case. "You know what's in here? A tape recorder. I made a trip uptown to rent this rig before I visited Tony. I've got a tape of everything Tony said to me. I dropped the tape into a mailbox before I came to see you. Any more questions?"

Moss puffed on his cigar. "I guess not." He looked up. "You'll cover me?"

"My only interest," I said, "is learning what happened to my brother. If you're not involved in his disappearance, you don't have a thing to worry about."

"Brother, smother." Moss sighed. "Okay. I know you won't believe this, but I'm really on your side. I have a kid brother of my own. But then this thing came up. An important client made a request. And what could I do? It didn't seem to concern how your brother disappeared. And if I went along, maybe he'd back me with the Clay Street newspaper."

"Which client is that?"

"It's a complicated story. At first it wasn't the client. You know who approached me first? George Nesbitt, the Journal reporter. He came up here and said, I just heard you handle the account for The Dugout where Kolchak lives. It's just possible Kolchak might learn something important about his brother. If he does, I want the story first. So if you find out everything he's up to, I'll see to it any releases you send the Journal about your clients get top consideration."

"He didn't offer money, though."

"No. That came later. When Joan and I paid a call on Phil Amber. I handle some of Phil's places, see..."

"I know."

"Well, I paid Tony five bucks a week to keep an eye on you. I'd relay everything Tony found out to Nesbitt. It paid off, too. I planted a lot of handouts in the Journal during that period. Then Phil and I got to talking about you. I mentioned I'd heard you just had lunch with Pete Ordway. Phil got real interested. So interested I told him how someone at the restaurant was watching you for me. Phil said, 'Marty, I'll pay you twenty a week for reports on Kolchak's activities. And a hundred if you can talk that kid into sneaking into his room, just to look at any letters or documents he might have lying around. That Kolchak can hurt everyone's business here and we wanna know what he's up to. If you do a good job, I'll consider your newspaper.' So I talked Tony into sneaking into your room for fifty bucks, and pocketed the other fifty myself. Amber was so pleased at what Tony found, he gave me another hundred. He told me to get Tony to go back up to your apartment at least once a week and to take notes on some of those documents in your closet."

"Did you tell Nesbitt about the documents?"

"No. I had to explain to Amber why Tony was watching you in the first place. Amber said not to give any more reports to Nesbitt, to give the reports only to him. So my deal with Nesbitt ended then. And when you moved out to that apartment building in the Second Ward, that goddam Amber called me up and said, 'Okay, Marty. I appreciate your help with Kolchak. But as for your newspaper—I had my investment analyst look into it, and the deal stinks.' Howdya like that?"

"Pretty raw. How much did Joan Engstrom know?"

"Only that Tony was keeping an eye on you for me. And that Amber paid me to get Tony to go upstairs and look around. What Tony found, I didn't tell her. She quit me, by the way. She's been sleeping with Bagwell and he got her a better job. But she's a real whore. Ronnie Layne gave me the story on her."

"You know Ronnie?"

"Sure. He's the only photographer in this neighborhood I can depend on. He told me yesterday, he took some pictures of Joan when she was in high school. She posed with no clothes on. What they call 'art' photos. And he laid her afterward. She sure made a jerk out of me."

"I wouldn't worry. Even if she has landed a job with a top agency, she won't hold it long if she can't produce. Not in that league."

"That's just it." Moss scowled. "Joanie's good. Better than I'll ever be. With half a chance she'll go all the way to the top." He stubbed his cigar out. "Excuse me. I'm going to lunch. With my wife and kids."

I dialed Max Fuller's office from a booth in Clay Drugs, the pharmacy owned by Pete Ordway's father. Max made me hang up and wait until he called back from a public phone. Ever since Captain Ware found Fuller's reports in my apartment, the private detective had been convinced his office and home phones were being tapped despite all his precautions.

"All right, Mr. Kay. You can talk now."

"Max, for what it's worth, I've learned Phil Amber knew all about your reports and everything else in my apartment. The press agent hired a spy."

"That's interesting, from a historical point of view. No doubt Amber told Schell. And when Schell heard you were involved in a rape case, he ordered Captain Ware to raid your apartment and make the stuff public."

"I'm thinking of bracing Amber. Just to verify that theory."

"You'd be a fool to try that. In the first place, even if you managed to see him, he wouldn't tell you the time of day. If you read the report I sent you on Amber you'd realize he's as tough as they come. You couldn't bluff the truth out of him, you couldn't trick it out of him, you couldn't beat it out of him. He's defied interrogations by experts, and you're no expert. In the second place, if you tried to force your way in to see him—and he'd make you do that—you'd give him the excuse he's waiting for. His boys wouldn't kill you. But when they were through working you over, you'd be a cripple for life."

"So where does that leave us?"

"You tell me." Fuller seemed in a testy mood.

"What's wrong, Max?"

"Dammit, I know you've got your troubles. But I suppose you have to be told. You'll read it in the papers tomorrow anyhow."

"The license revocation?"

"That's right. I thought when they dug up that old case, I'd have enough pull to kill it. But it doesn't look that way now. The mayor has much more influence with that board than my friends do, and the mayor has taken a personal interest. One of the mayor's subordinates as much as told me that city hall will drop the case if I stop working for you. And if I don't stop, the mayor will put me out of business for good."

"I'm sorry, Max. It was my fault for getting involved with the CGL. Under the circumstances, we'd better terminate our relationship. I have no right asking that you lose your license to practice on my behalf."

For a moment Fuller was silent. Then he said: "I'm afraid I'm glad you said that. Unless the client turns out to be a crook, I never leave a client except at the client's request or when the job is done. I don't like running out on you and you deserve all the help you can get. On the other hand, I know damn well that if I can't practice my profession, at my age I'll die of boredom inside of a month."

"Send me a final statement, Max."

"Why don't you come in early next week, and we'll make a settlement then. There's still a chance in a million I can block the revocation. I'll visit a few people over the weekend. But I don't really think it'll do much good."

Fuller hung up. I had more than a suspicion I had just lost my secret service.

When I left the telephone booth, Pete Ordway waited at the soda fountain. He grabbed my arm and steered me to a back table.

"My secretary saw you come in here," he explained. "Didn't you get the phone messages I left at your apartment building?"

"I did, Pete. But I got you in enough trouble already. You and the CGL too."

"Oh, hell." Pete's father brought us two cups of coffee. "Thanks, Dad. Listen, I know the CGL gave you a raw deal, disclaiming any connection with you. I wanted to go to the Clay Street Precinct that night and represent you, but the CGL wouldn't let me." Ordway looked down. "They told me that if I helped you, I'd be involving the CGL in a dirty rape case. They'd fire me from the CGL and I'd lose all the private business I was picking up from there. They said it in a polite way, of course, but that's what they meant."

"I'm not sore at you. Or the CGL either. I'm of age. The error was mine, in allowing my sympathy with your cause to interfere with my search for my brother. My private detective checked into you and the CGL, and you came out just as true and blue as you'd presented yourself to me. So I have nobody to blame for what happened but myself."

"Sure. But I want to make it clear." Slowly Ordway stirred his coffee. "Personally, I think the way we let you down was rotten. It was our idea you take all those documents. I got real sore that night. At the CGL. But when they put the screws to me—I had to give in. I worked hard, putting myself through law school. And now my whole future as an attorney and in politics is tied up with the CGL. I've got a wife and kids to think of. That's why I chickened out on you."

"You couldn't have represented me better than Harry Bagwell did. In fact, with all due respect to your ability, I don't think you could have matched his performance."

"That's not the point. I still worry about what you think of me, see. The way the CGL viewed it, it was worth stabbing you in the back to keep their skirts clean. I didn't agree. But I was overruled. And disillusioned."

Ordway stuck a pipe in his mouth. He filled it and fumbled for a match. He couldn't find one, so I handed him a matchbook from my pocket.

"Anyhow, I've made my confession. I feel better." He puffed. He glanced at the matchbook's cover. "That's my bank. The Midtown National. You bank there too?"

"No, I picked up the matches somewhere."

"My only consolation is, the CGL is still a far cut above the crowd around Hiram Schell and the mayor. One of the CGL directors got mixed up in that expressway land scandal, but no group's perfect. How's it going?"

"The search? Hard to say. On the surface, nothing's happened lately. But one thing leads to another. The watch, the credit card, the attack on Irma. The ring, the clothes, Mexoil. It's just a matter of plugging away."

"What's Mexoil?"

"A brand of motor oil. The police haven't made it public yet, but stains were found on some of my brother's clothes, and an oil refinery research lab identified the stains as Mexoil. Mexoil isn't marketed here any more, but a discount chain sold a big batch in the city a couple years ago at give-away prices. One of the stores in the chain is on Clay Street." I showed Ordway the label. "Ever see anyone with a can of this stuff lying around? Or an old can now being used to store nails in a basement or on a garage shelf? This Aztec design, black on orange, stands out like a sore thumb."

"No, I never did. The police learn more about who raped that girl?"

"Not a thing. They assume the attacker left by a back door leading to the alley. But they have no more suspects."

"I'm still inclined to go along with the police," Ordway said. "I think a bum who just happened to be in the building attacked her. But if she teas attacked because she was helping you, I can name one man capable of dreaming up a trick like that. Specifically, our mutual friend Phil Amber."

A letter postmarked Fond du Lac, Wisconsin, lay in my mailbox.

Upstairs, I opened it.

Dear Steve [Irma wrote],

It was good to hear from you. You must have gone through lots of trouble to learn where I am. I know my father isn't telling anyone. I wanted to write you earlier but didn't, I don't know why. Don't feel bad about what happened. I'm all right. I don't blame you for anything. Nobody knows me here. In a way it is a good thing. I am meeting new people and seeing new places and I like that. I suppose after a while I will get bored, like when I was at the bakery, but I'm not bored yet. I love my father but it is good to get away from him too. I'm afraid he would never understand that. I got a job as a checker in a supermarket. I lost twelve pounds and am out of doors a lot and everyone says I look real healthy. I apologize for my father hitting you when you tried to see me at the hospital. He means well. I hope you go on looking for your brother and find out what happened to him…

I tossed the letter onto a coffee table. I stared out the window.

Irma had been the first casualty in my little army. After the attack on Irma, I'd ordered Betsy and her cavalry out of action. And now Max Fuller was hors de combat. The only full-time soldier left was Sam Alban.

That was serious enough, but the war chest was running low. I'd been spending more money than I'd anticipated. My paying Bagwell two hundred dollars instead of five hundred wasn't just a matter of principle. That extra three hundred would have hurt. I estimated I could finance my current operations for maybe a few more weeks. Then I'd have to get a job and look for Ed part-time, or move into a Clay Street flophouse.

CHAPTER 15

Sam Alban adjusted his rimless glasses on his broad nose. He turned the ignition key and spun the steering wheel. We rolled out into the street fronting my apartment building.

"We gonna visit stores that sold Mexoil again?"

"Not today." I settled in the back seat of Cab 444. "I'm going to a birthday party in a suburb called Hill Acres. A house at 623 Crescent. Think you can find it?"

"I can find Hill Acres. It's off the North Freeway. But we'll have to ask directions to the house. The streets there go in circles. Who's giving the party?"

"Lorene. For Jackie."

"It must be rough on her now. With her old man laid up."

"It is. Your friends spot any more Mexoil cans?"

"Five more locations. I found one of 'em myself." Sam pulled a penciled list from his shirt pocket and handed it to me. Briefly I glanced at it. Only one location was anywhere near Clay Street. I returned the list to Sam. "Five locations don't sound like much," Sam added. "But my guys have been canvassing every basement and garage in their neighborhoods where old oil cans might be lying around, on their own time. There just ain't many Mexoil cans left in town."

"That's all right. Every lead helps. With half a hundred cab drivers on the prowl, we just might turn up something. Doyle will check out those locations. If any of the people involved look like live prospects, the crime lab will go over their cars, looking for traces of blood or anything else that might be a link to my brother's murder."

"I'm meeting a driver for another cab company this afternoon. His guys are looking too. I might have more names to add. I'll drop the list off at your building tonight. Incidentally, I made a big mistake yesterday. I took a fare down to Clay Street. Before I could get away, I got ticketed for double-parking and for blocking an arterial street."

"How much?"

"Ten bucks."

I gave Sam ten dollars.

"I'm sorry," he said. "The next time I drive into Hiram Schell's ward, I'll cover the numbers on my cab. That's illegal, too. But at least I'll have a fifty-fifty chance of driving out without a ticket of some kind."

We reached Hill Acres by noon. It took another fifteen minutes to find Lorene's house. Sam got lost three times. A small boy on a bicycle finally put us on the right track.

Lorene waited on the front lawn, waving. Sam parked in front of the dwelling, a modest split-level about ten years old. Lorene wore a white blouse and a form-fitting pair of brown slacks. She smiled. Lines of fatigue fanned from her eyes.

"I thought I'd better stand out here," she said. "I was afraid you'd go by. The street numbers are hard to see."

"They sure are," Sam agreed. He had fallen into a surly mood. Getting lost three times had hurt his pride.

I paid the fare and climbed from the cab.

"Sam, why don't you join us for a minute?" Lorene invited. "It's a warm day. There's some beer in the icebox."

"Thanks, but I better not. Can I hit the freeway on the street?"

"No. It dead-ends. You have to turn around and go back the way you came."

"Goddam. Who could remember that?"

As Sam pulled his cab into Lorene's driveway, six small boys piled out of the open garage door. Abruptly Sam braked to avoid hitting them. The boys ignored Sam and ran toward us. One of them hollered, "Hey, it's my birthday. I got a road race. Can you make it work?"

Jackie had light brown hair and Lorene's eyes and nose, complete with bump. His square chin was an inheritance from his father.

"I'll try," I said. "What's wrong?"

"We can't figure out the wires."

"Mr. Kolchak will wire your road race after lunch," Lorene said. "We're all starved. So let's join the girls in the back yard."

The boys ran on. Lorene and I started after them.

Sam's cab still sat in the doorway. Then, slowly, he backed out. As the cab straightened, I turned and waved. Sam didn't see me. He crawled by at about fifteen miles an hour, no doubt pondering how to find his way back to the freeway leading to the city.

It occurred to me, as the cab disappeared around a corner, that I should have tipped Sam more. He'd have to drive back to the city without a fare.

Guests were still arriving. Lorene introduced them, but in general they ignored me. Jackie displayed mild interest when I handed him his present, a plastic model kit of a Colt Peacemaker. But an impromptu wrestling match distracted him.

In the kitchen I removed my coat, rolled up my sleeves, and helped Lorene make hamburger patties.

"You have a nice home."

"It's wonderful for Jackie. He can go to school out here with his new friends. I don't worry about him if he's out alone. It's a long drive to the city, but for Jackie's sake I don't mind making it every day."

"What do they say about your father?"

"Even if he comes home, he'll be an invalid."

"How much longer do you think you can go on this way? Doing the work of two people, seven days a week?"

"I don't know." She brushed a strand of hair from her eyes. "I hired an assistant manager, but I can't expect him to take the interest in the business I take, or put in the hours I do. I was ready for anything but this—Pop's getting sick, leaving me alone with the whole enterprise. I'm finding out it's quite a burden. But my gosh, never mind me. What about you?"

"About the same. Only half the places on Clay Street throw me out now. Thanks to Schell and Phil Amber."

"Real nice guys."

"Yeah. I drive out on the Capitol Freeway now and then. In the off-chance of picking up a lead to my brother's body. And practically every cab driver in town is looking for Mexoil."

"Never heard of it. Sounds like a cosmetic."

I smiled. I told her about Mexoil. "Doyle's checked about twelve people known to have had the stuff so far," I added. "Until now, nothing. But Sam has a list of some more locations, and I'll give those to Doyle tonight. Were trying to keep this out of the newspapers as long as we can, so don't tell too many people."

"Mum's the word." Lorene winked. "And now, friend, the bad news. I'm behind schedule. So while I put the finishing touches on this potato salad, you're going outside to broil hamburgers. The briquettes are already warmed up. Think you can handle it?"

I charred a few burgers but nobody seemed to mind. Everything I cooked was consumed. The guests were sloppy eaters. One dropped a hunk of birthday cake in the bean pot. Nobody minded that either.

After lunch I wired up the road race, laying it out on the rec room floor. The little cars buzzed round the figure-eight track like grounded hornets. It was all great fun until a guest stepped on a car and squashed it.

"It's busted!" Jackie howled.

"We'll get you another car," Lorene said consolingly. "Hey, how'd you kids like to play croquet? Get the set, Jackie, we'll organize a tournament. And if any of you kids have to go to the bathroom, go through the garage and use the one down here. I don't want you tramping dirt on the carpets upstairs!"

The kids began tearing the lawn apart with their croquet game. Lorene gazed at them for a moment through the kitchen door. Then she turned and walked slowly into the living room. She pulled the drapes on the picture window. She sat down on the sofa.

"That'll hold 'em," she said. "For nearly half an hour."

She closed her eyes. She leaned her head back. Awkwardly I sat beside her.

The top two buttons of Lorene's blouse had become undone. She didn't seem to care.

"I should be out in the yard with 'em," she added. "It's Jackie's birthday. But I just can't. I wish I could send them all away. To a movie or something. But the kids can't walk to a movie from here. The movie is too far away. I have only one car here, Pop's car is down at the restaurant, for running errands. It would take all afternoon to ferry those kids back and forth from the movies. So we can't do that. I'm very tired. More tired than I've ever been in my life. All I want to do now is be alone with you. For just a quiet hour or two. For that little time, I could forget everything else. Pop, the restaurant, the payments on the cars and on this house. I've decided I need that now, to forget. With someone like you. You understand?"

"I think so."

"Then what are you waiting for? Kiss me, at least..."

She responded with uninhibited passion. Her arms encircled me, her hands dug into my back.

Then she rested her head on my chest. She closed her eyes.

"Stephen, I know it's wrong. With the children out there. My own son."

"I'd be taking advantage of you, Lorene. You might not think so much of me afterward."

"I knew you'd say that. We could, you know. The doors are locked. There's a bedroom a few steps from here. You could undress me, I'd undress you. If we love each other, nothing we'd do in there would be a sin, would it? As for afterward—I'm not a little girl, Stephen. I might not feel so ashamed afterward as you think."

"Would you be unhappy, Lorene, if we didn't go into the next room?"

"Of course not." She smiled. "I'm happy that you want to wait until we're really alone. It will be so much better. But for now just hold me. No man has done that for such a long time. And if you change your mind about waiting—I'll understand."

At five o'clock Lorene sent the kids home. She and Jackie and I walked into the attached garage and got into her car. Lorene took the wheel and Jackie was in the middle.

"We've just got time," Lorene told Jackie, "to pick up another road racer from the store before it closes." She looked at me. "Would you mind, Stephen, if I dropped you off at the railroad station? There's a suburban train to the city in fifteen minutes. Jackie likes to eat early Saturday so he can see his favorite television shows. If it wasn't his birthday, I'd drive you, but..."

"Sure." I looked at Jackie. This was the first chance I'd had to talk to him.

As Lorene started the car, I asked, "You ever do much traveling, boy?"

"Not much. I did when I was a baby. My father was a pilot. Do you travel a lot?"

"Stephen is an engineer," Lorene explained. "He goes all over the world. He builds bridges and dams. All sorts of things."

"That must be fun. I'd like to go all over."

"Maybe," I said, "you will one day. Lorene, when will I see you again? I still don't think it would be wise for me to show up at the restaurant."

"I wish you'd change your mind about that. I wish—I wish very much you'd move back upstairs. We don't have another tenant yet."

"I can't take the chance."

"Very well. I'm still afraid to leave the restaurant in a stranger's hands, Stephen. People who go there regularly expect to see Pop or me."

"You can't work sixteen hours every day."

"I'll have to." She sighed. "You know what Pop's doctor told me? He said, 'You better take a few days off. Get on a train, bus, or plane to some-place where nobody knows you, and just rest. If you don't, you'll be in here beside your father.'"

"That's a good idea."

"I might do that before I go back to work. It would give me a chance to think. All of a sudden, I have a lot of things to think about.

The deskman at my apartment building checked my mailbox. But Sam Alban hadn't dropped off his list of Mexoil owners yet. The electric clock on the wall registered six fifteen.

I rode an elevator to my apartment, picked up the telephone, and dialed Don Collins' number. I didn't have anything special to say to Don. I just wanted to invite him down for a drink. I wanted to talk to someone, anyone, to avoid thinking what I'd been thinking on the train.

Don didn't answer.

I hung up. I had to think anyway. About all the time I'd spent looking for Ed, and how I still seemed a million years from the answer. Could I have gone wrong somewhere? I couldn't see how. I had done everything a man could do. I'd questioned people in every dive on Clay Street. I made myself a permanent fixture down there, so anyone with information to impart could find me.

I brought Irma to Clay Street, to determine if she could recognize any-one. She didn't—and Doyle could be right. A perfect stranger, acting on a warped, momentary impulse, could have attacked Irma.

I'd even checked every newspaper printed a week before and a week after Ed disappeared. I'd probed every abnormal death or unexplained occurrence. The newspapers were still piled in a corner in the bedroom.

Thumbing through the newspapers, I had run into a few familiar names. Hiram Schell dedicated a playground a block off Clay Street the day before my brother vanished. Harry Bagwell lost a case a day earlier; he'd defended one of Phil Amber's hoodlums, accused of assaulting a customer who had protested a bill in one of Amber's joints. Amber himself, three days after the disappearance, refused to testify on grounds of self-incrimination before a Congressional rackets hearing in Washington. Pete Ordway, on the day of the disappearance, held a press conference at CGL headquarters and announced the county sanitary district had let a river-clearing contract to a firm headed by the mayor's son-in-law. Don Collins, four days before the disappearance, was named one of the "Ten Young Men on the Way Up" by the city's Chamber of Commerce. Martin Moss, a day later, was appointed publicity chairman of a committee formed to promote Dollar Daze on Clay Street. And on the morning my brother disappeared, George Nesbitt broke an exclusive series of articles in the Journal on narcotics sales to teenagers, especially in the Clay Street area. His prime source for most of his information was Captain Ware. The same edition of the Journal earned an account of how Doyle, at the head of a squad of detectives, raided a heroin den in a back room of a pizza parlor.

But while some names were familiar, nothing seemed to fit a pattern. I admitted to myself, at long last, that I was getting absolutely nowhere. And that perhaps I rated as the biggest fool on God's green earth...

I reached for a cigarette and the telephone rang.

"This is Kolchak."

"Steve? Van Doyle."

The lieutenant had never called me "Steve" before.

"Yeah, Van. I planned to drop in at the precinct later with a new list of Mexoil can locations from Sam Alban. The list is probably downstairs at the desk now."

"I don't think so."

"What do you mean?"

Doyle paused. "Steve, I wish I didn't have to tell you this. But your friend Sam Alban, he's dead."

Silently, I huddled in the back seat of a squad car headed into a part of town I'd never seen before. The neighborhood was mostly residential and declining, much like the neighborhood around Bronson's bakery. The patrolman at the wheel kept his mouth shut and his eyes on the road. By the time we pulled up to the police barricade, it was beginning to get dark.

A block ahead, alongside a coal yard, I saw Cab 444 parked alone by the curb.

Van Doyle opened the squad car door for me. A homicide detective named McGovern, who worked out of the uptown police headquarters, was with Doyle.

They led me to the cab.

"I came out here as soon as I heard about it," Doyle said, "because of Albans connection with you. Your brothers disappearance is still my case. He disappeared in my precinct during the hours I was in charge. I knew how close you were to Alban and that's why I called you. But I don't think there's any connection."

"You don't? What happened?"

"Some kids found him in the cab," McGovern said. "The body's already on the way to the morgue. It's plain enough. His wallet and everything else is missing. It happens to a few cab drivers each year. A cabbie picks up a fare. The fare orders a ride to a spot where nobody can see what happens, like here. The fare kills the cabbie and takes whatever he can find. Nine times out of ten, a job like this is pulled by a dope addict who needs a few bucks for a fix."

"What time was he killed?"

"As best we can tell so far, late this afternoon."

"When you went through his pockets, did you find a list?" McGovern frowned. "What kind of a list?"

"You'd know a list if you saw one." I walked around the cab. "Sam had a list in his shirt pocket. Locations where Mexoil cans were seen."

"He didn't have anything in his pockets," McGovern said. "His killer took everything."

I looked at Doyle. "How about that? First Irma Bronson. Then Sam Alban. And Sam's list of Mexoil locations is missing."

"It could have happened that way," Doyle said. "There's no second-guessing a junkie."

"This time you're kidding yourself. No junkie stole Sam's list. Sam Alban was murdered for only one reason. Sam was on my team. And he was close to something or he wouldn't have had to die. Thirty minutes ago I was about ready to throw in the towel myself. But not any more."

Sam Alban had many friends. When I arrived Sunday evening the funeral parlor was jammed. I paid my last respects. Alban's wife and two sons looked at me and I looked at them. There didn't seem to be much to say.

Two news photographers took my picture when I stepped outside. A light rain had started to fall. A boyish reporter I didn't know asked me a question but I brushed him aside.

George Nesbitt of the Journal followed me down the street "Hey, Kolchak," he called. "No hard feelings, right? I know he was a good buddy of yours. I'm sorry it happened."

I stopped and turned.

"Thanks."

"A miserable thing. Leaving the wife and kids. That's always the worst. The hundreds of times I've interviewed the bereaved, I never can get used to it."

Cautiously, Nesbitt moved closer. He seemed sincere. Probably he was. I still disliked Nesbitt, but I didn't intend to punch him again. He'd taken enough knocks in his life already. Fuller's investigation had disclosed that Nesbitt was an alcoholic, a diabetic, and a widower. He lived alone in a cheap hotel a few blocks from his newspaper. He had one daughter, a lush herself, who had run off with a door-to-door salesman to California. She didn't even bother sending Nesbitt Christmas cards, much less a letter now and then. Nesbitt was his publisher's pet, for scoops obtained decades earlier, and it was common knowledge on the Journal that Nesbitt would be eased into a dead-end desk job as soon as the elderly publisher died, which would be any time. The Journal's news executives didn't approve of Nesbitt's often vindictive tactics any more than the city's other crime reporters did.

"I been talking to some of the other cab drivers," Nesbitt said softly. "They tell me Alban was helping you look for something called Mexoil. The cops won't discuss it."

"Neither will I."

"I've been around long enough not to break a story that would compromise an investigation into a homicide. No cop in town would ever give me the time of day again if I ever pulled a bush stunt like that. I wouldn't print the story until Doyle or McGovern gave me approval. And maybe I could even help you find this Mexoil stuff. You think Alban's murder had something to do with your brother?"

"I'm sorry," I said. "I have absolutely no comment now. And if I ever do have anything to say, you and your publisher can read all about it in the Beacon."

I pulled my hat down and walked away.

CHAPTER 16

It rained all night and most of the next morning.

At eleven o'clock the sun came out. I left the apartment building and began hiking west. I had no destination. I wanted only to get as far from my telephone, which had been ringing constantly, as I could.

At a diner, I had coffee and a sandwich. And a little after four I walked into the Clay Street Precinct Technically, Van Doyle wasn't supposed to report until eight. But I found him in his office.

Doyle looked up with mild surprise.

"Where've you been?" he asked. "I just talked to McGovern. He said he tried to call you twice this morning and you didn't answer."

"I was in. I just didn't want to talk to anyone for a while. But that's all over now." I pulled up a chair. "What have you learned?"

"Still feel the same way?"

"You bet."

"I wish you were right." Doyle shuffled papers. "It would make things easier. We could try to tie everything together. But cab drivers lead hazardous lives. What happened to Alban…"

"Skip the lecture. I don't suppose your underworld informants have come forward yet with a tip about the dope addict you assume is responsible."

"It's still early."

"Uh-huh. Your Clay Street informants drew a blank when they looked for Irma's attacker too, didn't they? What about Sam?"

"Alban was shot at about four thirty in the afternoon. The body was discovered a little after six, but that spot is so isolated, the time lag isn't surprising. He was shot once, in the back of the head, with a thirty-eight-caliber bullet."

"You learn where he went after he dropped me off in Hill Acres?"

"Yes. He was last seen picking up a fare in front of the Moreland Hotel."

"Who was the fare?"

"We don't know. The doorman looked and noted that Alban had reached the head of the line. He looked again and Alban was pulling away. He had the impression a man was in the back seat, but Alban took off so fast, he couldn't be sure. He's positive the passenger was a pedestrian, though. Not someone who walked out of the hotel."

"That's just dandy. The Moreland—the one place Sam checked in several times each day at least to get messages from me. The place anyone could find him. The driver in the line behind Sam see anything?"

"No. He was working a crossword puzzle. But before you jump to conclusions, there's a chance the person who entered Alban's cab in front of the Moreland was not Alban's last fare. Alban's trip tickets were missing, too. Alban could have left that person off and picked up someone else at a different location. Were issuing a plea in all the newspapers and on television for the person who entered the cab in front of the Moreland to come forward."

"Some chance of that. Your crime lab go over 444?"

'They did. They picked up everything loose on the floor and under the back seat, too."

"For instance?"

Doyle reached for a paper on his desk.

"Well, the lab found seven hairpins, a box of condoms, two ball-point pens, a lipstick, a cigar in a cellophane wrapping, a pocketknife, a garter belt, fifty-seven cents in change, six empty matchbooks, and three matchbooks with matches still in them."

I had a thought.

"Any of those matchbooks," I asked, "from the Midtown National Bank?"

"As a matter of fact, yes. A new book with just two matches torn out. Why?"

"No definable reason. Only if I were you, I'd tell my crime lab to pay particular attention to that matchbook."

"They'll be thorough with everything. Do you happen to remember any of the Mexoil can locations on the list Alban showed you? If you don't, we can canvass the drivers and reconstruct it."

"I'm afraid not. But Sam told me he spotted one of those Mexoil cans himself."

"In that case," Doyle said, "we'll probably never know who owned that can of Mexoil."

I telephoned Max Fuller from a booth in a cigar store. I woke him up at his home.

"Mr. Kay, Max. I'd planned to come in and see you. But I wasn't up to it."

"I understand. My sincerest condolences. I don't trust this phone, give me your number…"

"It doesn't matter. Unless your efforts over the weekend were successful."

"They weren't."

"Very well. I hereby terminate your services. Send me your final bill at your convenience. If anyone overhears that, I don't imagine it'll get you in trouble."

For a moment Fuller was silent. Then he said, "I wish it could be some other way. Especially after what happened to the cab driver."

"You think he was killed for helping me?"

"I distrust any and all coincidences. First the baker's daughter. Then the cab driver. Doyle's no fool, he's probably coming around to that conclusion too. Only he'd never admit to such a far-out theory until he's collected the evidence to prove it."

"Speaking of coincidences—what kind of an outfit is the Midtown National Bank?"

"Eminently successful. It's not the biggest bank in town, but it's well-located, across the street from the commodities exchange building. It's also favored by lawyers, judges, and politicians because it's a block from city hall and the county courthouse. On paydays you can find a lot of newspapermen there; the Journal, the Express, and the Beacon all draw paychecks on the Midtown. And the city's biggest brokerage firm has its boardroom off the Midtown's lobby. You might say that while the Midtown's customers aren't the wealthiest men in town, they make the most interesting conversationalists."

"Thanks. One last favor. I want you to learn where Sam Alban's widow keeps a bank account, so I can add something to it without telling her until it's done."

"Of course. Kolchak—my running out on you this way—it's not going to stop you, is it?"

"Hell no."

"That's good. I wouldn't want to be the man to do that. And while I'm not on your payroll any more, feel free to continue asking my assistance whenever you need doors opened. Any more Memphis Clubs or what have you. And never forget my advice. If secrecy is involved, always call from a public phone. Never go through a switchboard. That may strike you as melodramatic, but the layman doesn't realize…"

"What did you say?"

"I said, it may seem…"

"Never mind. Thanks again, for everything."

I hung up. I stepped out of the booth, bumping into a man who had been waiting to get in. He scowled but I ignored him.

Slowly I walked around the block. The sudden readjustment in my thinking was so massive that its full implications did not become apparent at first. Then I realized that only one conclusion was possible. The Master

Plan had not failed me; I had failed it. But I was catching up fast now. Evidence should not be hard to find.

I walked around the block a second time. The third time around, I stopped at a tavern.

The bartender came over and said, "Look, buddy, I know you. You're not gonna bother my customers...

"Oh, shut up," I snapped, "and bring me a beer. I wouldn't waste a minute on the slobs in this place."

He brought the beer. I drank that and ordered another.

I said, "And I thought I was on the run. They're so scared, they panicked. But first, I'll learn where the body is..."

"What's that?" the bartender inquired.

"Nothing that would interest you. Where's the phone?"

I reached Bill Totten in the Beacon's city room.

"This is Kolchak, Bill. I wonder if you'd do something for me. I can't explain why now, but I promise that when the time comes, you'll get the story exclusively."

"Ask away."

"I've been following your expressway land scandal stories. I note you mention a lot of tracts along the route are held for unknown owners by bank trusts."

"That's right. As a matter of fact, I'm working up a separate piece on that topic. How an abnormally high number of properties along the route were purchased by trusts during the last three years—more than during the previous fifty years.

"Could you get me a list of every parcel along the route held in trust by the Midtown National Bank?"

"I could, but it would take time. The route crosses several counties. Each county maintains its own land title records."

"Well, how about starting with the portion of the expressway route nearest to the Capitol Freeway?"

"Okay. The expressway will intersect with the freeway in Boone County, where the River Road turnoff is now. The Boone County records will cover the route fourteen miles east and twenty miles west of the intersection point. I'll phone our stringer correspondent at the Boone County Courthouse and have him compile the list for you. He should have it ready by early tomorrow afternoon."

"Swell."

I hung up. I made one more call, to an automobile rental agency. I reserved a four-door sedan for eleven o'clock the next morning.

The car bounded up a country lane a mile south of River Road and two miles east of the old Flyways Airport. It was late afternoon. The land here was rocky and wooded: too barren for productive farming, too dreary and lacking in navigable water for resort property, and too far from arteries of transport to attract industry. This was scrubland, much of it going to waste. The suburbs had not reached here yet. No builder in his right mind would tie up his capital optioning unimproved acreage here in the faint hope of future development. And so the land lay cheap and unwanted—except by informed investors who knew in advance the route of the new expressway.

I braked before a wooden gate in a barbed-wire fence. The faded letters on the rural mailbox said HOOTEN. I checked my list. A sixty-acre parcel owned by the August Hooten Estate had been sold twenty-six months earlier to the Midtown National Bank and Trust Company as Trustee, Trust No. 4683. The parcel lay seven miles from the intersection of River Road and the Capitol Freeway, and sixteen miles from the ravine where Ed's possessions had been found. It was the third parcel on my list of eight. The first two had been vacant land in full view of River Road. The possibility of disposing of a body on either of those tracts had seemed remote, but I had searched them anyway.

I turned off the engine and climbed out of the car. Beyond the gate, a the track, rut road wound out of sight into a clump of trees. The area between the gate and the trees had been meadow once. Now it was a ragged, untended field.

A lock hung from the gate. While the gate was old and splintered, the lock was shiny and new.

With both hands, I grabbed the gate and pulled myself over. I began hiking toward the trees. At every step I stirred hordes of crickets. A big cloud moved across the low sun. Ahead, birds signaled my approach. I reached the trees and moved into shadows.

And then, beyond the trees, the cottage came into view. Unexpectedly it loomed on a rise about thirty yards distant. Small but of relatively recent construction, it seemed in good repair. The lawn had been cut, the shrubbery pruned. In front of the cottage, someone had parked a black, two-year-old Cadillac.

I glanced to my left. Just beyond the trees, at the foot of the rise where it would not mar the view from the cottage, a pit had been dug. The occupant of the cottage dumped his trash and garbage there. The remains of a small fire still smoldered on top of the pit, which was loaded with ashes, rusted cans, charred paper, and dozens of empty liquor bottles. That's how you disposed of trash this far out in the country. You burned it, and then buried it.

I went on. The drapes on the cottage's picture window had been pulled wide. I peered in, at a living room furnished cheaply but tastefully. Newspapers littered the floor. An empty glass lay overturned on a coffee table.

An ash tray beside the glass overflowed with cigarette butts. On the wall, an ancient, double-barreled shotgun hung over a print of a hunting dog. From the room's dimensions, I estimated that the cottage contained at least one bedroom in addition to a kitchen and bath.

I reached for the doorbell. But a clinking sound from behind the cottage caused me to change my mind about pushing it. I turned and walked around the side of the cottage. The lawn muffled my footsteps.

The land immediately behind the cottage had been equipped as a patio area. A few reclining canvas lawn chairs circled a barbecue pit. His back to me, a man sat in one of the chairs. He was leaning forward, pouring himself a drink. He set the bottle down on a metal table and raised his glass.

I said: "Hi, Harry."

The lawyer twisted his neck and stared. He wore a sports shirt and rumpled slacks. He needed a shave. The hand holding the glass trembled. But his eyes seemed as canny as ever.

"Hello, searcher. How in hell'd you find me? Bribed my secretary into telling you about this place, I suppose. You must be in real trouble to track me down way out here. What are you accused of this time? Or have you decided to pay the three hundred you owe?"

I lit a cigarette, with another match from the Midtown National.

I said, "I'm not in trouble, Harry. You are." I glanced around. "Nice place. You come out here often?"

"In summer. That's what the previous owner built it for—a summer home. I bought it for investment."

"I was sure you bought something out this way. You were never known to pass up a sure thing before. And what could be surer than the expressway route?"

Bagwell chuckled. "As a matter of fact, it develops that the parcel is rather well located. I've already entertained two offers. But I've discovered the place makes a nice retreat. Where I can get away from all those idiots in the city. I pay a farm kid to cut the lawn once a week during the season. But whatinhell you mean, I'm in trouble?"

"I mean," I said, "that you killed my brother Ed, slugged and raped Irma Bronson, and then murdered Sam Alban."

"I think you've flipped. You've been continent too long." Bagwell tossed off a slug of bourbon. "What you need is a willing woman."

He said that, but the old fire wasn't there. At the end, his hoarse voice broke and sort of faded away.

I sat on a lawn chair. I stared at the attorney and said: "The last one was different, wasn't it, Harry. You had to plan Sam Alban's murder. You had to see him and talk to him, knowing that in a few minutes you'd kill him. Probably you were stone sober at the time, which is why you're so busy keeping drunk now. You really don't have the stomach for it. There's still enough decency in you to make you recoil at the idea of premeditated homicide. I bet you drove right out here after the murder and have been trying to drown yourself in booze ever since."

Bagwell frowned. "You seem pretty sure of yourself." He twirled his glass. "But hell, it's too ridiculous to discuss. I had no motive for doing any of the things you're accusing me of doing. And you have no evidence…"

"When I tell the police what I think, they'll collect evidence easily enough. Let's take Sam Alban's murder for a start. That was a hasty job. You were rattled and like most murderers, you made mistakes." I held up my matchbook. "You dropped one of these. Matches from the Midtown Bank. Each time I see you I wind up with a packet of these matches in my pocket. You must leave 'em on tables and bars wherever you go."

"Sure, that's my bank. I pick up matchbooks whenever I'm in there. But a million other people can get the same matches."

"Yeah. But I bet you don't remember dropping the book in Sam's cab. And maybe when the crime lab looks it over they'll find particles on it, matching particles in one of your pockets. Or even a great big fingerprint. Who knows? And when the police search your apartment and this cottage, they might find the clothes you were wearing when you murdered Sam, with blood on them maybe. Or gloves, with traces of nitrate. Also, you're a man of distinctive appearance. The trail is still young. The police or I will find someone, somewhere, who remembers seeing you the afternoon Alban was killed. Seeing you loitering in the park across the street from the Moreland, waiting for Sam's cab to come along, or seeing you leave the neighborhood where the cab and the body were found. How about an alibi for your whereabouts Saturday? You got one?"

Bagwell didn't reply.

"I thought not. I don't understand you, Harry. A man with your background getting involved so deeply that you'd commit a premeditated homicide—a first degree. You, of all people, know the risks and the consequences. My brother's murder must have been an impulse of the moment. The attack on Irma—you didn't hit hard enough to kill, and knowing your filthy mind, I imagine you thought you were doing her a favor when you raped her. But Sam Alban—why in heaven's name did you go through with that? Or was killing him Lorene's idea?"

Behind me, in a flat voice, Lorene said, "That's right, Stephen. It was my idea."

Lorene stepped from the back door. Her hair was disheveled, her face fearful and determined. She wore sandals and a short blue lounging jacket that ended a few inches below her hips.

In her hands she carried the shotgun I'd seen on the living-room wall. The barrels were pointed at me.

"Face front," she ordered. "Lean back. Put your hands flat on the chair arms."

I obeyed. Sunk deep in the canvas chair, I wouldn't be able to rise without giving plenty of warning.

I glanced at Bagwell. "How'd she persuade you, Harry, to kill Sam?"

Bagwell rose. He picked up his bottle and moved out of the line of fire. "Self-preservation," he said heavily, "was a motive, of course. And Lorene knows my adolescent weakness for the flesh. I told her I'd murder your cab driver if she came out here and performed certain personal services for me. She didn't like the idea—but I must say, she's more than kept her word." He gazed over my shoulder. "How much," he asked Lorene, "did you hear just now?"

"Enough."

"He's got a point. My print could be on that matchbook. I dropped the gun down a sewer, but the clothes I wore when I shot Alban are still in my apartment. There's blood on them. When I ran from Alban's cab, I turned a corner and almost knocked over two small girls playing on the sidewalk. If the police ever consider me as a serious suspect, we could be in a jam."

"They won't consider you," Lorene said, "if Stephen doesn't talk to them."

Bagwell shook his head. "I don't know. Each time we commit a crime, our risk of detection increases. And the more crimes we commit, the more severe our punishment will be when we are detected."

"Are you chickening out, Harry?"

"Oh, no." Bagwell flashed a malicious grin. "But I'm not going to make the decision this time. This time, Lorene, well see if you are up to it. You've taken charge of our strategy. All right, pull the trigger yourself. After that, I'll help you. But you'll have to kill him if you can. So you'll know how it feels to take a life in a calculated way."

"I'll do it. You'll see, I'm not afraid." Lorene walked around me. She stopped in the shade of an oak tree. The shotgun was an indistinct, black object pointed at my midsection. But Lorene's bare legs and intense features, taut with apprehension, were quite discernible.

"Get up," Lorene said to me. "I loaded both barrels. My husband was a skeet fan, and I can shoot. At this distance, I couldn't miss. Put everything in your pockets on the ground. Then sit down."

I rose. "Bagwell's right," I said. "It isn't easy to kill a man." I began emptying my pockets. "And the police will track me here anyhow."

"I have to kill you," Lorene argued. A ring of desperation tinged her voice. "I'm not going to give up everything now. I've worked too hard and risked too much. Nobody is going to take it away, not from me and not from Jackie."

"It's not Jackie you're thinking of. You've grown used to that nice house in the suburbs. And the two cars, and the big paycheck every week."

I sank back into the chair.

"Harry, get that stuff," Lorene said.

Bagwell wandered over. He kneeled and gathered my possessions. I considered jumping him. But Lorene seemed so near the edge of hysteria, I feared she'd kill both of us.

The attorney straightened. He walked to the barbecue and leaned against it.

"The usual junk a man carries," he mused. "But he's got a list here. Expressway properties held in trust by the Midtown National. He's checked two properties and mine's the third. Which means, to begin with, he wasn't precisely sure what he was looking for. And being a secretive fellow, he probably didn't tell anyone what he was up to. He's got a receipt from a U-drive. He must have parked by the gate.

"Very well," Lorene said. "After I shoot him we'll put him in the trunk of his car. I'll drive it to the city, park near Clay Street, and walk away. The police will think the underworld killed him, for nosing around Syndicate dives on Clay Street. That's a Syndicate technique, isn't it? Shotgun a man, put his body in the trunk of a car, and then abandon the car?"

"That's good," Bagwell conceded. He reached for his bottle. "Still…"

"Dammit, Harry, there's no choice."

"Lorene," I said. I spoke facing her. But I addressed my words to Bagwell. Something about his attitude convinced me he represented my best chance for survival. "Before you kill me, think it through. What I figured out, others can figure out. I came here today. Doyle and his detectives will be here tomorrow, or the day after. Commit another murder and you'll create a whole new set of circumstances to trap you. It's got to end somewhere."

"If the police come," Lorene said, "they'll think you just looked around and went back to the city. None of the natives saw us. I'll clean this place up before we go." She licked her lips. Her lower jaw trembled slightly. "Stephen—when you found us here, you didn't seem in the least surprised."

"I wasn't. Finding you was an unexpected bonus. I was looking for evidence my brother's body is here, so I'd have something tangible to present to Doyle. But I knew if anyone was out here, it would be one or both of you."

"I want you to tell me how you knew. You do that, Stephen, and we'll tell you what happened to your brother. And you'll die on your brother's grave. That way, at least, your search will be ended."

CHAPTER 17

Bagwell appeared shocked at the callousness of Lorene's proposal. Intently he gazed at her. Then he tipped his bottle and drank deep.

"I don't mind telling you," I said, "so maybe you'll realize it's just a matter of time before Doyle or Max Fuller or someone else reaches the same conclusions. When I came to this city, I had a Master Plan. I'd be the front-line troops, so to speak. I'd make myself conspicuous on Clay Street, questioning everyone I met. But I really didn't expect many good answers. That was part of the act. My Master Plan was—if I nosed around long enough, sooner or later, the people who knew what had happened to my brother would get curious about my activities. They'd be dying to know what, if anything, I had learned. And one way or another, they'd try to find out. I figured if Max Fuller, my secret service, checked everyone who displayed even a remote interest in me, sooner or later I'd have a file on the killers. And if I kept studying those files, a pattern would emerge. And I'd be near the truth."

"I thought that was it," Bagwell said.

"Sure. And my plan worked. Actually, I should have seen the pattern months ago. But Lorene dazzled me. No man can be entirely objective about an attractive woman when he thinks she's falling in love with him. And so I didn't see the pattern until yesterday, when Fuller reminded me about his telephone precautions. Then I remembered, I'd observed his precautions on important outgoing calls, but not on some incoming calls. One, in particular. The call Irma Bronson made to my apartment, to set up our last date. I told her I'd treat her to a stroganoff dinner. Nobody but Irma and me knew in advance we'd made that date. The only way anyone else could have known was by tapping the phone. Now, Harry Bagwell knew all about arranging for tapped phones. He'd been involved in a wiretap scandal, for which he'd nearly been disbarred. And when I thought of you in that light, Harry, things began to fall into place. You, your relationship to Lorene and The Dugout, and all the rest of it."

"Actually," Bagwell said, "the tap was in a closet in Lorene's office. A tape recorder was activated whenever you picked up your phone. Your apartment was bugged, too. We couldn't have been more overjoyed when you accepted Lorene's invitation to move upstairs."

"No doubt. It occurred to me yesterday that Lorene's interest in me was out of character. Until I came along, she'd never warmed to any man except her late husband. Lorene the Iceberg, the Jaycees called her. Could she have been attracted by my good looks? My vast wealth? Hardly. Lorene kidded me and I'd kidded myself. It also occurred to me that The Dugout prospered mightily just after my brother disappeared. In walks Harry Bagwell with a party of friends. A total stranger, who samples some stroganoff and then runs off to find investors for a costly restaurant venture. Or so the story goes—and I'm sure you staged that visit, Harry, to explain your sudden interest in the place. I suspect The Dugout was mostly your investment, with the other guys in for peanuts."

Blandly Bagwell nodded. "I own nearly ninety percent."

"Right. But backing The Dugout wasn't in your character as an investor. Opening an expensive restaurant on Clay Street is like shooting craps. All your past investments had been sure things. Real estate where you knew values would go up. Stocks where you possessed inside information. And your new restaurant wasn't doing so hot. Week nights, it was half empty. Lorene had to rig a full house for Jerry Gourmet. Moreover, Lorene wasn't the best of restaurant managers. She made more goulash and chop suey than necessary. Her father began drinking on the job, sure suicide for a restaurant greeter. But you kept pouring money into The Dugout nevertheless. All in all, it smelled of a payoff. A payoff for what? Almost certainly, if you were tapping my phone, for concealing the facts about my brother's death. And if you were paying off, Harry, it meant you killed my brother."

Bagwell looked away. But Lorene's eyes never left me.

"It would have happened," I went on, "in the old Dugout. A clean, quiet little bar, two blocks from Clay and Jackson. The sort of spot where my brother would stop first, to ask questions about the new town. At the hour he probably arrived, on a cold week night, the cook and waitress would have gone home. And it was also the sort of spot where Harry Bagwell might stray on one of his lone, nocturnal wanderings. Bagwell the lecher, in a foul mood because he'd just lost a case. Bagwell the bully, the insulter, who when drunk flew into rages and once blackened a bar girl's eye. My brother couldn't stand seeing people pushed around. If you tried something when he was present, he'd call you on it. And I think that's what happened. Somehow Bagwell, in a rage, killed Ed. And the weapon Bagwell used to kill Ed is the key to what happened later. Harry, I think you did it with the bayoneted World War I rifle Lorene's father had hanging on the wall."

The silence proved I'd been right.

"Ed was bayoneted to death. That's why Lorene dropped a tray of glasses the first time she saw me. She thought I was staring at the bayonet, not the portrait under it. And that's why Ed's body had to disappear. Because if it were found, any journeyman pathologist could have recognized a bayonet wound. And Doyle or any other detective in the Clay Street Precinct would recall a bayoneted rifle hanging in a bar two blocks from where Ed was last seen."

I closed my eyes. I took a deep breath. "After that—Bagwell, you persuaded Lorene and her father to help you get rid of Ed's body. In return, you backed the new restaurant. Ed's pockets were emptied in The Dugout. You drove the body here and stripped it. Even if you didn't dispose of it right away, it would be safe on your property for a few days. Going back, you detoured at the ravine, twenty minutes distant, to drop off Ed's clothes and ring. You probably knew about the ravine because you defended a maniac who killed two teenagers there once, the sort of front-page case you love."

Bagwell nodded. "Stanley Witkowski. A vastly misunderstood boy."

"Yeah. The ground was frozen and you didn't do a good job of burying Ed's clothes. But that was okay. The main thing was—years later, if anyone found what was left of Ed near the cottage, they wouldn't find any personal effects to make an identification. Not even a button. And if Ed's stuff was found in the ravine, the police would waste weeks looking for a body that wasn't nearby. So you were all set until I came along and found the watch at Bronson's Bakery right off. Who dropped the watch, Lorene? You or Jackie?"

"Jackie," Lorene said. "He attended a private school then, two blocks from there. Pop gave him the watch without telling me. But it seemed ordinary enough, and I didn't have the heart to take it away…"

"I think I know the school. I used to meet Irma in front of it. And of course when you saw the sign the Bronsons put up, you were afraid to claim the watch. You knew Ed's name would be inside; you probably never entered the bakery again. But let's go on, to the first time we met. To cover your panic at seeing me stare at the rifle, you threw me out as a Clay Street bum. But that gave you an excuse to invite me back later, to learn as much about my activities as you could without seeming to try. It was easy. Hardly anyone else in the city had been nice to me. You were doubly nice. When I needed a place to live, you provided one—with built-in telephone taps. The morning I awoke and found you beside my bed, you weren't there because of concern for me. You were prowling my apartment. And one day your telephone tap really paid off. You heard Irma agree to stake out Clay Street with me. Then Irma and I made that last date. You knew I'd take her to The Dugout afterward, which would have been disaster. You might not be there, Lorene, but Irma would see your picture on the wall. And recognize you as an old customer."

"Lorene," Bagwell said, eyes on the ground, "hinted I should kill the girl. But I told Lorene I knew another way to discourage her."

"Didn't you, though. If you'd been tapping the phone, you knew about our security precautions. We worked them out on the phone. What did you do, Harry? Rent an office down the hall and then wait until Irma was alone?"

"Not down the hall—across the hall. In the name of a little land company I own. And if I failed in stopping the girl, Lorene's father was set to take the picture down, on grounds that vandals had defaced it. You're wrong about one thing. I'm not proud of what I did to Irma Bronson. But the incident served its purpose."

"Yes, you scared Irma off. And you spilled booze around and tossed dirty pictures into the wastebasket. Just enough details to make sure I'd be held for questioning. In the process, I'd be tarred in the newspapers, so Phil Amber would feel free to bar me from his joints. And you could pop up later as my attorney, to learn firsthand what was in my mind. But you didn't know Amber had his own spy system. Nor that Schell would order Captain Ware to raid my apartment. The bad publicity I got from that worked in your favor. But Schell forced me to move out of The Dugout. You couldn't tap my telephone any more; Lorene's insistence that I remain was quite sincere. And there was another unhappy development. Lorene's father suffered a heart attack. He'd been cracking all along, that's why he started drinking so much. The assault on Irma finished him."

"He's old," Lorene said. "He won't fight any more…"

"Perhaps. So what happened? I left The Dugout and kept plugging. And now you were so curious to know what I was up to that Lorene asked me to her home. To meet Jackie, she implied. But actually to establish a basis for later, more intimate meetings, where my confidences would be complete. Now, when I arrived at the house in Hill Acres, Sam dropped me off in front. Then he pulled into the driveway. The garage door was open, the lads ran out. Sam paused there, a good ten or fifteen seconds before he backed into the street. Why? He'd been looking all over town for Mexoil cans. And I think he saw one or more in that garage."

"There were four," Lorene admitted. "On a shelf. Holding bolts and things."

"One can or four, Sam would have no trouble spotting them. The Aztec design stands out like a neon sign. After Sam left, I told you about Mexoil. You realized why Sam drove by the house so slowly. He was about to add your name to his list. So you sent me out to broil hamburgers. You hid the cans Sam had seen. You called Harry Bagwell and persuaded him to murder Sam. Later that afternoon, you made sure I didn't get bored with a kid birthday party. That gave Harry plenty of time to find Sam before I returned to the city. It was a convincing performance, Lorene…"

"That's enough." Lorene looked at Harry. "The police would find evidence if he ever told them what he told us. Even if Pop didn't crack under questioning, and he would. But nobody suspects us yet. So you see why it's necessary."

"I told you before. It's your decision."

Lorene looked back at me.

"Stephen, you'll never understand. I never loved you. But I grew to like you. I don't want to kill you. But I absolutely must…"

"Just one thing," I said. "What did happen to my brother?"

Bagwell said, "I guess you're entitled to that." He tipped his bottle and drank again. "Like you figured, I was drunk and mean, the only customer in the place. Then your brother came in. Heineman was out back. I hollered for a drink and Lorene brought it. She was so damn frosty and superior, I couldn't help getting fresh. She slapped me. I knocked her down. Your brother tried to interfere. He shoved me against the wall, then kneeled to see if Lorene was all right. I reached up and tore that rifle from its mountings. Like every ex-Marine, I knew about bayonet fighting. I lunged. I realized immediately I'd gone too far, but I was too off-balance to stop. Your brother was still on one knee, turning to face me, when I ran him through. If it's any consolation, he died almost instantly."

"It is."

"I understood then that my moment of drunken rage could ruin me forever. I couldn't fix this mess by bribing the victim. Lorene was still on the floor, staring at me. Her father returned, took one look, and started for the phone. I said, 'For God's sake, before you call the police, hear me out. I'm a wealthy man. Help me get the body away, and I'll reward you.' Lorene's father wasn't interested. But Lorene was. She made me show her my wallet. She took my cash and said, 'All right, Mr. Bagwell. I'll make you a sporting proposition. You put up the money for a first-class restaurant here. If I can make it succeed, you give me the restaurant when your investment is paid out. If it fails, you absorb the losses and my father and I go on collecting nice salaries. Is it a deal?' It was. We dragged the body into the kitchen. Lorene ran a mop over the floor. Her father cleaned the bayonet and put the rifle back on the wall. All this took just a minute. When the next customer walked in, John was behind the bar as usual. Out back, Lorene and I emptied your brother's pockets—that was her idea, she wanted the money in his wallet too—and loaded the body into the trunk of her car. I drove Lorene home first so Jackie's sitter wouldn't get suspicious. Then I drove here, stripped the body, and covered it with brush. It would keep until the weekend. On the way back I dropped the clothes and jewelry at the ravine. I parked near Lorene's apartment and caught a bus home."

"The body, Harry. How did you dispose of it?"

"Over the weekend, I dumped it in the garbage pit. I covered it with junk, doused the pile with gasoline, and put a match to it. What was left, I buried down there. No crime lab could tell anything, except it had been a man once."

"So now you know," Lorene said to me. "Stand up. Let's get going."

Slowly, I walked down the rise. Lorene trailed about five yards to my rear. Bottle in hand, Bagwell trailed Lorene.

The attorney, I began to realize, was not going to lift a finger to help me. His earlier disquiet had evaporated. He seemed entirely satisfied now with the way things were working out.

We reached the garbage pit. It was nearly dark. A few embers still glowed. Ed's bones were under those ashes somewhere. At least I'd learned what I'd come to learn. I knew what had happened to Ed, and who had done it to him.

"Turn around," Lorene ordered.

I turned. Lorene stood several yards from me. Bagwell was far to my right, walking slowly, still holding his bottle. Thoughtfully he viewed Lorene.

"Lorene," I said, "I'm not pleading. I'm just telling you. Go through with this, and they'll get you for sure. Give yourself up, and you'll still have a chance to live."

"I'll risk it." Lorene raised the shotgun to her shoulder. Her eyes were wet but unblinking. "Stephen, I wish you hadn't interfered. But nobody is going to interfere. Not the baker's daughter, not the cab driver, not even you…"

I tried to make a break then. I thought that if I rolled away and she missed with the first barrel, I could reach cover before she could aim and fire the second.

But I never had a chance. As I threw myself to my right, she pivoted, keeping me in her sights. She delayed just a second, weighing my life in her mind for the last time.

Then her finger tightened on the trigger. The gun detonated. The booming report crashed against my eardrums.

Pellets tore into my legs. But incredibly, the weapon had exploded not so much at me as in Lorene's face. Shrapnel flew in all directions. The main force of the blast was directed backward.

Lorene was knocked sprawling.

She lay still.

I crawled to Lorene. A fragment of the gun's action had been driven into her skull. For Lorene, it had been a lucky fragment. Her face had been cut to a pulp. And had she lived, she'd most certainly have been blinded.

Bagwell limped to my side. He sat down.

"Lorene's husband," he observed moodily, "may have taught her to load, aim, and shoot, but he didn't teach her much about guns. That weapon was an antique. It hasn't been fired in more than forty years. It was made for relatively mild black-powder loads. The barrels were fouled, rusted, and full of obstructions. Almost any shell would have blown up in the chamber. And the shells Lorene inserted—they're tailor-made, high-powered loads, designed for a weapon that cost me four hundred dollars, which I keep in town unless I'm going hunting."

The lawyer took a final swig of his bourbon.

"I was going to tell her," he added, "but I changed my mind. When you found me here today, I'd already given up. I understood, even if Lorene didn't, that our deception was doomed. Doyle would get us if you failed. But until now I'd done all the dirty work. I killed your brother, raped the girl, and murdered Alban. The state would ask the chair for me. Lorene, though, she could claim I was behind everything and get off with no more than a few years. This despite the fact that from the moment she got off the floor in The Dugout and stared at your brother's body, she ran the whole show. So I thought: Let's see, Lorene, if your greed has so warped you that you'll commit your own murder. If it has, you'll squeeze that trigger and get your punishment. If it hasn't, you'll put the gun down and surrender, in which case a few years in prison and lifelong heartache for yourself and Jackie will be punishment enough. That's real justice, Kolchak. She was her own executioner. As for you—I knew you'd be hurt some. But with her aim thrown off and the pellets dispersed by an explosion in a bad gun, I was reasonably sure you'd survive. And I feared that if I warned her, she wouldn't have believed me anyhow. She'd just have fired at me first."

"Harry," I said, "my legs…I can't move any more…"

"Oh, I'll call the police." Bagwell looked out at the woods. "I think I can beat the chair by describing Lorene to any reasonably male jury. I'll go to the state penitentiary where the warden is a friend of mine. So are many of the inmates. In a few months, I'll be running the place. And there are, I've learned, worse places in the world to be than a well-run penitentiary."

CHAPTER 18

Doyle perched on a chair in my hospital room. He watched as I limped to the closet and reached for a necktie.

"I'll give you a ride to your apartment," he drawled, "in a squad car."

"Thanks."

"If you like, I'll turn the siren on."

"That won't be necessary."

"I wouldn't mind. I couldn't say it before. You were making monkeys out of us, and my pride wouldn't let me. But I think you put on a helluva good show. Too bad everything worked out the way it did."

I tightened the knot.

"Everything worked out the way it had to work out. I did what I came to this city to do. What's too bad?"

"Steve, after what you've been through, you must have a pretty lousy opinion of the human race. Leeches trying to suck you dry. Lice like Nesbitt and that photographer hurting you out of sheer spite. Rats like Amber and gray wolves like Schell hurting you out of greed. And the woman your brother died for tried to blow your brains out with a shotgun."

"That's one side of it," I admitted. "But there's another. Total strangers went out of their way to help me because they were decent people. Guys like Sam Alban, the Moreland doorman, and the cabbies who helped look for Mexoil. Betsy and her friends. Irma Bronson. Don Collins and Max Fuller. The old rascal, I learned he'd been charging me half what he charges other people all along. And for every Nesbitt, there are a hundred reporters like Totten. That balances the picture, doesn't it? By the way, what will they do to Lorene's father?"

"He's in such poor health they won't press charges. Anyhow, Lorene and Bagwell did everything against Heine-man's wishes. Bagwell's trial starts next month. He'll fight for a life sentence—on what grounds, he hasn't disclosed yet.

"Think he'll get the chair?"

"He might get sentenced to it. But the governor is against capital punishment. And Bagwell still has friends close to the governor's mansion. If anyone's death sentence gets commuted to life, Bagwell's will."

I reached for my coat.

"What about Jackie?"

"Ward of the court. He's the biggest tragedy."

"It might have been worse still," I said, "if he grew up under Lorene's influence."

The telephone rang. Doyle picked up the receiver. "Mr. Kolchak's room. Uh-huh. Just a minute." He looked at me. "It's Pete Ordway."

"Tell him," I said, "I've just left."

"He's just left," Doyle said into the phone. He hung up.

"That's about the tenth call from that guy," I said. "He wants me to write articles for the Beacon on my impressions of Clay Street. I've got nothing against Ordway. In fact, I admire him."

"You have a lot of company. He'll be alderman one day. Schell can't live forever. And then…"

"I agree. He'd make a good mayor in about twenty years, wouldn't he? But my articles wouldn't have much effect on his political future. And I'm damned if I'll let even a man like Ordway capitalize on my search. Because I came here, a good man was murdered; a woman was beaten and raped; a mother is dead and a child has been orphaned. No matter how good their intentions, nobody's going to cash in on that."

Betsy waited outside my apartment. On her last visit to the hospital, she'd learned I was coming home that afternoon.

I opened the door and Betsy lugged my suitcase in. I flopped into a chair.

Betsy kissed my forehead.

"Cut it out," I protested. "I keep telling you…"

Betsy straightened. "You mean because you're older, you don't want me?"

"It's not that I don't want you. It's just that it would never do."

"Steve, you're as young…"

"As I feel. But when I feel fifty, you'll feel thirty-three. You'd be surprised what a difference that makes. And when I'm sixty…"

"Don't say that." Betsy frowned. She sat on the sofa. Her eyes brimmed with tears. "The desk clerk said you were leaving."

"That's right. Tonight. I have to start living my own life again."

"Take me with you."

"If I were ten years younger, I might, but…"

A knock sounded on the door. I opened it. Don Collins joined us.

"Hi, Steve. Just wanted to wish you luck. Where are you headed?"

We shook hands. "Thanks for everything, Don. I sent a few wires from the hospital. A construction firm based in Omaha wants to see me. They have a big job in Afghanistan."

Betsy, her back to us, began to sob.

Don asked, "What's wrong, hon?"

"Shut up," she said. "And don't call me 'hon.'"

"She's upset," I explained vaguely. "Look, I've got a lot of packing to do. My plane leaves at seven. I'll spell out my gratitude by mail. But for now, why don't you two run off somewhere? If you want to say good-by at the airport, fine." Betsy left without a word. Hastily Don followed.

I peered out the window. A minute later Betsy and Don emerged from the building. They had effected some sort of reconciliation during the elevator ride downstairs. Hand in hand they walked to Don's sports car. Don whispered in Betsy's ear. Betsy giggled. Don patted Betsy's fanny, and Betsy hopped into the front seat.

If they showed up at the airport, I'd be very surprised. And disappointed.

One well-wisher attended my departure.

Max Fuller, the private detective, lumbered into the waiting room as my flight was called.

"Hey, boy," he bellowed. "Before you go—I still think you were a damned fool. But a few more damned fools like you and this would be a more interesting world."

"Thanks. I got your letter, with the name of Mrs. Alban's bank—and your donation to her account. But what happened to your final statement?"

"Didn't I mail it yet? Well, I'll send a bill eventually." Fuller sighed. He pulled a handkerchief from his pocket and mopped his brow. I'd never seen him standing up before. He was much shorter than I'd thought. No more than 5'5". A little old gargoyle. "Going back to building bridges, hey?"

"That's right. But before I sign up for the next job, I'm flying to Wisconsin. I want to know the Bronson girl better. From her letters, she's trying hard to keep her chin up, but I suspect she still feels pretty bad about what happened. She's a nice girl, Max, with a lot to live for. And she's a smart, realistic girl who could move to a place like Afghanistan just like moving next door. A real boomer type. She doesn't realize that yet, but I do."

"Well," Fuller said, "happy landings."

The jet engine whined. I leaned back in the seat. We headed up and away. I didn't look down.